PRAISE FOR ZACK DELACRUZ: ME AND MY BIG MOUTH

"Zack Delacruz prefers to stay in the background. He knows that being noticed will only lead to trouble. After a school assembly on bullying, Zack decides to stand up for a fellow classmate and in the process gets roped into being the lead fund-raiser for the school dance (if he and his classmates sell enough chocolate bars, they'll be allowed to attend the dance for the first time). Zack goes from flying under the radar to being the center of attention. Things go well until someone eats several of the boxes instead of selling them, leaving Zack to pick up the pieces. Though characterization is light, Zack's class is a diverse mix of students. Zack is a relatable narrator and embodies the middle school experience. The steady pace makes this novel a solid pick for reluctant readers."
— *School Library Journal*

"Anderson's debut children's book stars sixth-grader Zack, who has perfected the art of being invisible in school—until he surprises himself by standing up to the class bully, José. . . . [Zack] is a sympathetic narrator, and Anderson spiritedly renders the voices and personalities of preteens. . . . The story does trace Zack's maturing and his class's bonding to a pleasantly satisfying finish."
—*Publishers Weekly*

"By book's end, [Zack's] a hero."
—*Booklist*

"By the end of the story, readers are going to be dancing. I'm sure of it."
—**Kathi Appelt, Newbery Honor author of *The Underneath***

"Zack and his crew prove that to survive middle school, you need street smarts, kind hearts, and some crazy, gutsy determination."
—**Wendy Shang, author of *The Great Wall of Lucy Wu* and *The Way Home Looks Now***

ZACK DELACRUZ

JUST MY LUCK

ZACK DELACRUZ

JUST MY LUCK

By Jeff Anderson

STERLING CHILDREN'S BOOKS
New York

STERLING CHILDREN'S BOOKS
New York

An Imprint of Sterling Publishing
1166 Avenue of the Americas
New York, NY 10036

ISBN 978-1-4549-2067-0

Distributed in Canada by Sterling Publishing
c/o Canadian Manda Group, 664 Annette Street
Toronto, Ontario, Canada M6S 2C8.
Distributed in the United Kingdom by GMC Distribution Services
Castle Place, 166 High Street, Lewes, East Sussex, England BN7 1XU
Distributed in Australia by NewSouth Books
45 Beach Street, Coogie, NSW 2034, Australia

For information about custom editions, special sales, and premium and
corporate purchases, please contact Sterling Special Sales at
800-805-5489 or specialsales@sterlingpublishing.com.

Illustrations and Design by Andrea Miller

Manufactured in the United States

Lot #:
2 4 6 8 10 9 7 5 3 1
08/16

www.sterlingpublishing.com/kids

For those who need to know it gets better.
(It does.)—J.A.

CONTENTS

Life is partly what we make it, and partly what is made by the friends we choose.

—Tennessee Williams

CHAPTER 1
BY THE SEAT OF MY PANTS

Alone in the noisy Davy Crockett Middle School cafeteria, I sat with my pepperoni pizza, my fruit cup, and my thoughts.

Only two weeks ago I saved the sixth-grade dance with a car wash. An eighth-grader called me Mighty Mouse, and the whole sixth grade cheered for me. But here I was, eating by myself.

You'd think *that* kid would be sitting at a table surrounded by friends. And they'd be laughing at one of his clever stories. But that's not what happened. Not at all. Don't get me wrong. Things did get better. I didn't try to disappear anymore, but it turns out that I was invisible whether I liked it or not. After all that had happened, I still only had one friend who'd eat breakfast and lunch with me—Marquis. But today he had a doctor's appointment for the ankle he sprained helping me save the dance. He wouldn't be back till tomorrow.

"Eat up!" Mrs. Gage, the cafeteria monitor, ordered like a military officer. At the next table, Cliché and Sophia rolled their eyes and swigged the last of their chocolate milk before carrying their trays to the wash station. The rest of their table followed, because the blue-eye-shadow gang mimicked everything that Sophia did. After eating, everyone returns their trays and goes outside to the blacktop. I try to avoid the blacktop. Lots of kids + a paved surface + one easy-to-distract teacher's aide = trouble.

To keep myself inside, I concentrated on eating slowly. Each time I took a bite, I counted thirty chews. One, two, three . . . When Marquis was gone, everything seemed to take longer—even chewing. Dad said I should "widen my circle," whatever that means. Dad asked me the other night: "Do you ever do anything without Marquis?"

"Uh, no." I shot back darts with my eyes. "He's my best friend."

"Best—not *only*," Dad had said. He didn't know how rare sit-by-you-at-lunch and talk-to-you-when-I-don't-have-to friends are.

From the tray to my mouth, I moved my Spork in slow mo. To keep my mind busy, I read the signs taped up on the cinderblock walls: FALL FIESTA-VAL THIS SATURDAY! Oh, brother. Next my eyes scanned to the à la carte line, which everybody calls the pizza line because nobody wants to say "à la carte." Can you blame them? But the next sign I read caught my attention. I had to read it twice:

TABLES ARE FOR EATING STUDENTS ONLY.

Tables are for *eating students* only.

I moved my lips as I reread the sign, scrunching my face up with disgust.

Seriously? That sign must be one of those "funny" errors Mrs. Harrington always talked about in English. To be honest, the whole sign is ridiculous because in all the time I've spent in this cafeteria, I'd never seen anyone "eating students" at these tables. Not even once. Not that I'm complaining. Seeing kids going full-on zombie, munching on brains or peeling off each other's skin like it was fried chicken, would totally skeeve me out.

"You need to eat and exit, sir!" Mrs. Gage paced and prodded, paced and prodded.

"I'm still eating," I pleaded, turning back to her, flashing my pitiful puppy-dog eyes. I was trying to give myself even more time to stay off the blacktop.

"Humph!" She rolled her eyes as if I'd offered her a cafeteria roll I'd found on the floor.

I wondered if Mrs. O'Shansky, the head cafeteria lady, had made the tables-are-for-eating-students sign. If she did, she ought to loosen her hairnet for more blood circulation to her brain. One thing's for sure, whoever wrote that sign didn't have Mrs. Harrington for English. That lady is all about "your writing making sense." You have to know what punctuation means. Especially when it's "published," and I know anything laminated is definitely published.

Fwam!

José Soto, aka El Pollo Loco, just finger-flicked my ear, zooming past my table on his way to the pizza line. Again.

3

"Very funny, José," I turned and said to everyone who was listening, which was no one. Just when I think El Pollo Loco and I are cool, he flicks my ear or trips me in class. The honeymoon-from-José harassment had lasted only a few short days after the dance. He, like the others, seems to have amnesia about how great we all were at the end of the dance, laughing and talking. I mean, they still talk to me. Like Sophia said hi to me in the hall the other day. It's just not how I expected. That's middle school: one day you're hot, the next you're not.

wwww

I chewed and chewed again while my mind chitter-chattered away. I was sporking up the last bit of my gray fruit cup pears when out of the corner of my eye someone captured my attention. I turned. A girl I'd never seen before stood at the end of my table. A new girl. She looked like she was from some far-off place. Maybe India or California or something.

Anyway, I always love it when new kids come to school because your past is washed away. They've never seen or heard of you. They don't know your nicknames or any of the goofy things you've done. You get a second chance. You can be somebody new—cooler, funnier, better looking. I sat up straighter just thinking of it.

Her eyes were grayish ice. I had never seen gray eyes like that before. And she stood a few inches from my table.

Problem was, the new girl was with the most irritatingly happy girl known to man: Blythe Balboa. Blythe was just elected the sixth-grade student council representative, and she is bossy—b-o-s-s, b-o-s-s-y. She always wears a cardigan sweater with way-too-long sleeves because she's freezing. "BRRRR" will be etched on her gravestone:

HERE LIES

BLYTHE BALBOA

"IT'S FREEZING IN HERE, Y'ALL. BRRRR."

Seriously.

If she doesn't freeze to death soon, I'd be surprised. Anyway, as student council representative for sixth grade, Blythe was the official introducer of students new to Davy Crockett Middle School. Blythe shows them around, pointing her sweater-covered hands at the gym and the library. I wondered if the most interesting girl with grayish ice eyes would be in my classes.

"That's the pizza line. Did they have those where you came from?" Blythe pointed her sweater stump to the left. "That's the regular tray line. Today, it's Salisbury steak, tater tots, and mac and cheese." Blythe stuck her sweater-covered stub up for a high five. "Starchfest!"

But the interesting girl shook her head "no." She wasn't having any of it.

"Oh, yeah, I forgot you're one of those vegetarians." Blythe nodded. "Principal Akins warned me."

Ooh, a vegetarian. I liked that. I mean, I didn't really like vegetables, but this vegetarian sounded cool.

"My mom's a vegetarian." The words escaped my mouth like a loud burp. The thing is, my mom isn't a vegetarian, but the counselor, Dr. Smith-Cortez, said, "One way to make friends is to find things you have in common." I didn't know anything else about her, so I'd have to go with vegetarian.

The new girl looked at me. She smelled like the candle aisle at the supermarket.

Blythe Balboa turned her nose up at me and spun away. "This way," Blythe wrapped her Balboa constrictor arm around the new girl and dragged her toward the pizza line. "À la carte's over here. We'll get you a potato. Don't worry, the Fakin' Bits aren't real bacon. I'll get one too." Blythe laughed. "We can be potato twins. I just LOVE potatoes— any starch really! Starch gives me so much energy. Oh! I could just about explode!"

And no one would have been surprised if she had.

The new girl looked back at me and cracked a tiny smile. The most interesting girl I'd ever seen in my whole entire life, and I made her smile. *Ca-Ching!*

Wait a minute. My mind chitter-chattered again: What's going on here? Why am I so interested in this girl? Why is she the most interesting? I didn't even know her. Still, I was interested. I had to talk to her. Now. It was important. Man, I wished Marquis were here to bounce this off of.

And then I heard a voice: "Just get up and go talk to her. You know you want to."

Was that my conscience calling? My conscience calls me sometimes—especially when I'm feeling nervous. But usually I let the call go to voicemail.

"Life is a banquet, and most poor suckers*ss* are starving to death!"

As the voice continued, I realized my conscience sounded an awful lot like Janie Bustamante.

I spun around. At the end of the next table, Janie—the movie line quoter—stood. *"Auntie Mame,* nineteen fifty-eight, starring Mrs. Rosalind Russssssssell." Janie crammed the rest of her Fudge-icle in her mouth, and pulled out the empty stick, pointing it behind me. "Six O'clock." Her voice was muffled by Fudge-icle, but I knew she meant for me to turn around.

"Hurry up or El is going to get to her first." Janie warned. She'd taken to shortening El Pollo Loco, José's infamous nickname, to El. I hated it. Basically, she was calling him "The." But for some unknown reason *El* was catching on with everyone else too. Anyhow, whatever you called José, he was bouncing up and down behind the most interesting girl, while she shook pepper on her potato. I thought about it. The new girl wouldn't know what a fool José was either. Janie was right. I had to talk to her first.

Both the confidence I'd gotten this year and the old panic flooded my body. I had to do it. I would stand up. I would walk over to the pizza line and talk to the new girl before El won her over. Ugh. Now, I'm calling him "The." I'd had enough; I jumped up from my stool.

RRRRRRiip!

Let me clarify. I jumped up. My pants? Not so much.

CHAPTER 2

TORNADO OF TROUBLE

The seat of my khaki pants, the whole backside above my legs, stayed attached to the stool, caught on a screw. Now my pants only covered the front of my legs and the bottom half of the back of my legs—just below my biscuit. (That's what Dad calls a butt. Don't ask.)

For the first time in recorded history, the Davy Crockett cafeteria was still and silent: no loud voices competing to be heard, no Sporks scraping against plastic trays, no movement at all. Everyone was suspended like in a photo. A sea of faces stared, eyes wide, mouths open. No one even let out a breath for what seemed like an embarrassing forever.

A chill raced up my spine when it hit me: I'd run out of underwear this morning, so I had worn my Champ the Choo-Choo Underoos from second grade. Dad doesn't get rid of anything—he says we can use old clothes as cleaning rags when we paint or something, but then we never paint anything. Anyway, it was either tiny Champ the Choo-Choos or some of Dad's nasty, baggy boxers, or commando. What would you have done?

I hadn't counted on my khakis catching on the stool.

The underwear had been so tiny it looked like I was wearing a thong. The thong song was playing in my head the whole way to school this morning. How could I forget?

Now I'd never be allowed to forget.

As the shock wore off the crowd, a tornado of comments spun around the cafeteria, picking up speed.

"That's so thong!" José called from the pizza line. "Nice *chones*, Dela-*loser!*"

Chones is Spanish for "undies," but some people say it means "girly panties." A funnel cloud of laughter and shouts whipped and whirled over the cafeteria tables.

"Oh, my eyes!" Blythe covered her face with both cardigan stumps.

My eyes shut too. I couldn't look at anyone. I wanted to sink through the cafeteria floor, far away from here.

Panicked, I attempted to outrun the tornado, but the lower half of my pants still clung to the stool. I was chained up like a pit bull in a yard, pulling and struggling to get loose from the stool. Everything blurred into the sound of the cafeteria laughing and pelting me with insults: "Thing a thong for us, Zack" mixed with "I saw something so thong" and "Zack ate Maca-*chone* and cheese." Swirling and twisting out of control, the tornado of embarrassment destroyed every bit of courage I'd gained this year.

With one final yank of my body toward the cafeteria exit, the rest of my khaki-covered legs tore free, leaving behind my dignity along with the frayed threads and part of my khakis that had once covered my swimsuit area.

My Champ the Choo-Choo biscuit was on full display as I fled toward the exit. Even though my Underoos were tiny, my hands were not large enough to cover them.

With a bang, I burst through the metal doors and sprinted down the long hallway without looking back. Faster than I'd ever taken laps for Coach Ostraticki, faster than José could scarf a pizza slice, I ran. The front of my pants flapped in the wind, exposing even more of me.

I would've raced all the way home, but by the time I sprinted out the front doors of the school, I was out of breath. I leaned over, hands on my knees, panting by the flagpole.

The hot sun warmed the bare back of my legs, and I did the only thing I could do—collapse on the sidewalk. My khakis looked more like a frayed tan blanket in my lap than pants. The only way to cover myself was to sit my biscuit on the hot sidewalk for the rest of my life.

Coach Ostraticki walked out the front doors of the building. "What's going on, Delacruz?" He twisted the ends of his curly mustache.

I tried to catch my breath. "We ran out of quarters for the laundry at my dad's apartment, so I had to wear some old underwear."

"It's a story as old as time, kid," He shook his head, staring up at the sky. "I know how that goes."

He leaned down and grabbed my hand and pulled me up.

"Here," He unzipped his black velour warm-up jacket and then handed it over. "Tie the sleeves around your waist."

"Thanks," I knotted the jacket arms like a belt. I shuddered as I realized his jacket was touching my underwear.

"Don't worry about it. I'll wash it later," he said.

I nodded.

"Too bad this happened on choo-choo train day, though, huh?" Coach O. smiled, lifting his mustache curls.

"It's Champ the Choo-Ch . . . never mind." I shook my head.

He led me and my black-velour-covered biscuit back toward the school. "You wanna know somethin'?"

I didn't, but I was sure that wouldn't stop him.

"The good thing about getting embarrassed is that it's already in the past. Trust me. You'll be laughing about it in no time."

He was right about that. There would definitely be *no time* I'd ever be laughing about this.

From the nurse's office, I called Mom and begged her to bring a pair of khakis for me fast—plus a plain white, roomy pair of underwear with maximum biscuit coverage. After I hung up, I sat on the squeaky bed in the clinic.

"You're having an exciting year, Mr. Delacruz." Nurse Patty pushed her glasses back with her index finger, smiling.

I nodded.

I really was having an exciting year—but not in the way I'd hoped. I sighed, wishing there were some way to make the excitement end for just a second or two.

But I knew better. This was middle school.

The clinic bed whined a long squeak as I leaned back against the cool wall, waiting for what would come next.

"**S**an Antonio, Texas, is a city of many colors—bright buildings and people of every shade." At least that's what it said in the *Explore Puro San Antonio* brochure I flipped through in Nurse Patty's clinic. The dull reading material helped me forget what had happened in the lunchroom. Maybe if I pretended the whole lunchroom khaki-tastrophe never happened, everyone else would forget too. Then, the whole horrible event would float into the sky like a helium balloon of embarrassment, farther and farther away till it disappeared.

I looked back at the fun facts section of the pamphlet. Maybe I could distract the most interesting girl from the *pantalone* problem by sharing fun facts about San Antonio. I studied the brochure like I had a big test coming up.

But by the time I'd memorized that San Antonio was the eighth largest city in the US, I came to my senses. No one would ever forget what happened. The Fighting Alamos would always remember this disaster. I imagined the headline in the yearbook: "The Day Zack Delacruz Bared His Biscuit to a Silent and Shocked Cafeteria of Innocent Bystanders."

Well, you can't blame a guy for fantasizing they'd possibly forget, even if only for a few seconds, can you? It was all I had left. A fantasy of some would-be, could-be, should-be life where my pants always covered my bottom and I only wore underwear that fit and didn't have choo-choo trains on them.

Sighing, I stared at the second hand slowly ticking on the clock above the clinic door. Every second I sat in the clinic was a lifetime. My biscuit still without permanent cover meant my nightmare continued. Any second a kid with a headache could burst into the clinic and laugh at me all over again.

Where was Mom? She was already out of the office when I called her cell. She'd said, "I'll swing by the store and drop off the clothes ASAP." She loves saying ASAP like one word. She's too busy to say "as soon as possible" or even say each letter. I was the one feeling like *a sap* for believing she'd come quickly.

I tossed the brochure on the bed beside me and sighed.

"Are you excited about the fall festival this Saturday?" Nurse Patty pointed to the poster that hung on the wall across from me: FALL FIESTA-VAL THIS SATURDAY: GET YOUR CASCARONE ON!

I shrugged. Sophia's mom, the PTA president, had changed the name from festival to *fiesta*-val because San Antonio loves the citywide Fiesta celebration in the spring. Mrs. Segura thought we should bring a little spring to the fall and sell cascarones.

She's right. Cascarones are probably the only reason anyone would want to go to the stupid Fall Fiesta-val. I love smashing the confetti-filled eggshells on my friends' heads. Cascarones are one thing everybody loves. Sure they're a mess. But that's half the fun . . . wait a minute. I could be the one who explains *cascarones* to the most interesting girl! That's it. I was so excited I momentarily forgot my pants situation and leapt up.

"Is everything quite all right?" Nurse Patty turned.

"Yes." I flopped back down on squeaking clinic bed, the rest of my pants falling a few seconds behind. "I hope so."

Cas-ca-rones. CASCARONES!

Now I had cascarones on the brain, which was better than *chones*. This year cascarones are guaranteed to be extra big at the Fall Fiesta-val. Blythe twisted every sixth-graders' arm into bringing at least two-dozen cascarones for a student council fund-raiser at the festival. She wanted 4,000 cascarones, so we'd have epic amounts of confetti eggs to bust over each other's heads.

I had been so excited about all those cascarones in one place, I'd invited Marquis to spend the night with me at Mom's house last Friday. We'd had a blast making ours.

wMMm

While Mom tended to the delicate egg surgery—knocking out a tiny hole at the top of each egg, draining, cleaning, and drying the flimsy shells without breaking them— Marquis and I made confetti. Sure, you can buy confetti at the store, but that's cheating.

Ca-click. Ca-click. We danced around the dining room table while we used a hole-puncher on construction paper and magazines—basically anything colorful and no longer needed.

"Don't make a mess, boys!" Luckily, Mom was so involved in egg surgery at the sink she was unaware of the zillions of confetti bits landing on the wood floor around the table.

Marquis and I shot each other a look. "That's what dust pans are for." I said.

Ca-click. Ca-click. Marquis hole punched over his head, like he was making dance moves.

"Make it rain!" I laughed. But as fun as Friday night had been, Saturday morning was even better.

At 7:00 a.m., Marquis and I dug into the confetti piles and dropped the tiny bits in the holes at the top of the empty eggs Mom had prepared yesterday. It took so much concentration dropping the confetti bits through the tiny hole I almost didn't notice Mom in the kitchen. She wore her pink warm-ups but no makeup. She opened the refrigerator. "Do you want scrambled eggs for breakfast and omelets for lunch and quiche for dinner?"

"Do we have a choice?" I asked, adding the last pieces of confetti to my fourth egg. That's the thing. When you drain two-dozen eggs, you have lots of eggs to cook. I tiptoed over and grabbed some grated cheese with my confetti-covered fingers.

Mom swatted my hand with a spatula. "Get back to work, Zack."

"This has turned into a sweatshop." Marquis whispered to me while gluing the tissue paper to seal his egg before resting it in the crate in front of him.

Those were the good times.

All it took to ruin the good life was a stool with a loose screw. Life is like that. One little thing changes it all.

~~~~~

"Hello, hello, hello?!" Mom tapped on the clinic door, jangling her keys, bringing me back to the present, back to the nightmare that my life had become. "Mom to the rescue." The door swung open, banging against the file cabinet. "I come bearing gifts." She held up pants on a hanger and a plastic sack like she'd just won a race. Her designer perfume filled the room. But not even her sweet smell could make this situation any better. "What on earth happened to you, Zack?" She looked down at my khaki shreds.

"Can we talk about it later, Mom?" I made my eyes big and motioned my head at Nurse Patty, who smiled and looked up from the papers she was filling out.

Mom thrust the pants toward me, still clipped on the plastic hanger, tags dangling. "This was the best I could do. I'm showing a house to a client in twenty minutes." She pulled a three-pack of underwear out of the sack and plopped the undies onto Nurse Patty's desk as if they were school supplies, not something that covered my swimsuit area.

"Mom!" I jumped up and swiped the underwear pack off Nurse Patty's desk.

Inspecting my backside, Mom asked, "How on Earth . . ."

Nurse Patty stood. "I'll give you two some privacy, Mrs. Delacruz."

"It's Murray."

"Oh, I sincerely apologize, Ms. Murray." Nurse Patty scooted her rolly chair under her desk.

"No problem." Mom handed Nurse Patty one of her business cards. "If you ever need to sell or buy a house . . ."

Seriously? How much does Mom have to embarrass me? It's bad enough she wears that gold jacket with her real estate company's name on it and slaps those obnoxious magnetic signs on her car doors like they're billboards. Now she's giving her business card to Nurse Patty, trying to sell her house. And what's up with Mom today? She put my underwear on Nurse Patty's desk. Who does stuff like that? Doesn't she know I was the victim of an *I-see-London-I-see-France-Everybody-saw-my-underpants* episode? And then to add crazy bread to the humiliation pizza order, she had to make a big deal that her last name isn't the same as mine, practically telling everyone she's divorced. That's right everybody! My parents aren't together anymore. I'm surprised Mom didn't rent the sign in front of the school to put the announcement in blinking lights.

Anyway, I grabbed the three-pack of tighty-whiteys.

"I only need one pair, Mom." I complained, ripping open the clear plastic with my teeth.

"Well, sweetie, why don't you take the others home to your dad's apartment so you have some for tomorrow and

Friday?" Mom leaned down and kissed me on the cheek.

"But I don't have my backpack" I whined. "It's in my locker."

"Zack," Mom whined back. "I think you can walk them to your locker without dying. Everybody wears underwear." With her thumb, she wiped her lipstick from my cheek. Her black heels *click-click*ed as she crossed the room to the door. "It'll be all right, Zack." Mom turned. "Call me tonight and tell me all about it."

You had to hand it to Mom. She took care of business.

CHAPTER 4
CARDBOARD KHAKIS AND A LOADED DIAPER

I wrapped my old pant shreds around my Champ the Choo-Choo underwear and then shoved it all in the trash, pushing it to the bottom. I had no choice but to put all three pairs of underwear on at the same time. I wouldn't be caught dead carrying tighty-whiteys down the hall. That'd get more attention than a live rattlesnake skateboarding through a ring of fire. Especially after already showing my *chones* to half of the sixth grade at lunch. Wearing three pairs of underwear didn't feel right—at all. But you do what you have to do in middle school, and I had to save whatever shred of reputation I had left.

The new khakis were stiff as cardboard. I adjusted several times, unable to get comfortable. I wondered if anyone would think I was wearing a diaper—a diaper with a load.

I traveled down the hallway to science, the khakis making a swish-swish sound. *Swish-swish. Swish-swish.* Great! Now I was also the kid who wore a full diaper under cardboard khakis. It just kept getting better.

In my head, I rehearsed how I was going to get the new girl to see me as something other than the guy who mooned the cafeteria. *Swish-swish.* I was back to The Fun Facts of San Antonio Distraction. I would overwhelm her with cool things she needed to know about San Antonio. Then maybe she wouldn't think I was such a dork. *Swish-swish.*

I'll tell the new girl stuff like how there's more than one way to say "San Antonio." Raymond Montellongo and his football friends write raps about "San Anto." Old men, like Grandpa and the announcers at the rodeo, say "San Antone." And the preacher at the church Mom makes me go to says, "Good morning, 'San Antonia'!"

I was almost out of breath rushing down the hall. *Swish-swish. Swish-swish.*

The science room door creaked louder and louder the slower I tried to open it. Everyone turned.

"Hey, he's back from his Zack Attack!" El Pollo Loco yelled. "Ah! Ha! HA!"

Everyone joined the laugh-a-thon.

"Did you get to the bottom of it, Zack?" Cliché Jones shook her head, laughing.

It was strange having Cliché make fun of me, since she likes Marquis so much. I guess even the shield of being Marquis's best friend didn't help anymore.

"That's quite enough!" Mr. Stankowitz, our science teacher, said. Brushing back the strands of oily black hair he combed over his bald spot, he turned to me. "Take a seat, Mr. Delacruz. You're just in time to meet our new student."

"I hear his *chones* met her at lunch," Sophia raised her hand for someone to give her a high five. "Don't leave me hangin'!" But the look in Mr. Stankowitz eyes was so strong it forced Sophia's arm to lower, inch by inch.

"Blythe." Mr. Stankowitz motioned for her to change the subject. "Let's get this show on the road. Please introduce the new student to the class."

"This is Abhijana Bhatt. Ah-Bee-Jon-uh Bott. Did I say that right?" Blythe looked back at Abhijana.

"Yes," Abhijana smiled. "But everyone can just call me Abhi." She pronounced it like Abby: A-b-b-y. Her eyes were even prettier than I remembered—gray and blue and clear. Sophia's flea-market contacts were no match for the real thing.

For some reason, all I could think about was Abhijana Bhatt. She was like no one I'd ever known—a vegetarian who smells like candles.

Even though she was wearing the same uniform as all the other girls, red top with a khaki skirt, her black hair was curlier and shinier and longer and newer. I got so lost in my racing thoughts that I missed Blythe's whole introduction of Abhi. I was so mad at myself for not listening, because there was nothing I was more interested in than Abhi. All I know for sure is Big Mouth Blythe said something that Abhi didn't like right at the end.

"But don't treat me any differently," Abhi said. "Please."

"Abhi," El Pollo Loco stood and spoke in a deep and breathy voice, like a tela-novella actor. "Welcome to our science class." He winked, twisting the ends of his nonexistent mustache. "I am El." He bowed like a combination of Prince Charming and a bullfighter. You could almost hear a trumpet playing.

Man, I was planning to be the one with charm. Who was this El guy?

"Abhi," I stood. "I welcome you to the whole school."

"Abhi," El stood again. "I welcome you to the whole city."

"Speaking of cities—fun fact—did you know there are several ways to say 'San Antonio'?"

"Abhi," José interrupted me. "I welcome you to our whole state."

"Fun fact—Texas used to be a country." I forced a smile.

"Enough, boys!" Mr. Stankowitz ended our Abhi standoff. "Thank you for the social studies lesson, but this is science class and we have other things to accomplish today."

I slapped my head. I should've led with the cascarones. What was I thinking? I had blown it again.

"I have an empty seat next to me," El said, raising his eyebrows up and down, tapping the empty chair.

"That's intentional, José." Mr. Stankowitz gripped the sides of his podium. "You need a buffer zone. And it's going to stay that way."

"That's quite enough," El mocked Mr. Stankowitz.

"Abhi, take a seat behind Zack," Mr. Stankowitz pointed.

I couldn't believe my ears.

"Hi," I whispered to her over my shoulder.

But she didn't say anything back, so I whispered louder.

"Hiii."

No answer.

She wasn't picking up what I was putting down. She's probably already decided I was a fool. I mean I had just bared my biscuit to the whole cafeteria. I don't suppose anyone could miss that—even if it was her first day. Besides kids like Sophia, who weren't even in the cafeteria, already knew what had happened. And Marquis wasn't here to stick up for me. I couldn't catch a break.

After that, Mr. Stankowitz got busy teaching about atoms and how they make up all matter.

"Sir," Janie stood, interrupting. "Matter is like—'The stuff that things are made of.'"

"Yes, Janie." Mr. Stankowitz nodded.

Janie whispered as she sat down. "Inspired by *The Maltese Falcon*, nineteen forty-one."

"Janie, we talked about this." Mr. Stankowitz warned. Teachers had been telling Janie to stop quoting movies during class.

"Starring Mr. Humphrey Bogart," Janie mumbled into her hand.

Mr. Stankowitz sighed.

"Nineteen forty-one? They didn't even have movies back then!" José shouted.

"Of course they did," Abhi chimed in. "I did a report on the history of movies at my school in Minneapolis. The first silent movies were made in the late eighteen hundreds, so movies have been around for over one hundred years."

Whoa! I had no idea what Abhi had just said, but she sounded smart, and she put José in his place.

"Where have you been all my life?" Janie stood again, gazing at Abhi.

"Janie, sit down." Mr. Stankowitz walked over to her desk.

Janie scribbled wildly, writing the name and year of the movie she just quoted.

"Please give me that." Mr. Stankowitz held out his hand.

Janie tore off the edge of the paper and crammed it in her mouth. "It was nothing." She swallowed.

I can't tell you for sure why Janie ate the paper, or how Abhi knew that fact, but I can tell you this, matter has more than one meaning. Like atoms don't matter to me right now. Not their nuclei made up of protons. Not their neutrons surrounded by electrons. And when Mr. Stankowitz tried to make the atom lesson more interesting by comparing it to a fried egg, he only made me hungry.

The only interesting part to me was how electrons are attracted to the protons by an electromagnetic force. It felt like an electromagnetic force was pulling at me to talk to Abhi. And the only thing that really mattered was convincing Abhi to talk to me. She's pretty and smart and put José in his place. She had everything.

When the bell rang, the electromagnetic force compelled me to try to talk to Abhi again.

"Do you need help finding your next class?" I turned toward Abhi's desk.

Her head was down, studying her schedule printout.

She didn't answer. She just kept staring at her schedule, her shiny black curls falling over her face.

Oh, man, that was cold. She was acting like she didn't even hear me. Mom does that sometimes when she's really mad—gives you the silent treatment. But what did I do?

Abhi looked up and flinched, as if she were surprised to see me looking at her.

José tapped her on the shoulder, and she looked right at him. "Where do you go next, Abhi?"

"I go to gy . . ."

Before Abhi could finish responding to José, Blythe Balboa scooped up the schedule and wrapped her sweater arm around Abhi and dragged her into the hall. "Let's go, Abhi. I'll show you the best way to get to the gym."

"Bye," I mumbled. But she was gone.

I walked over to the door and watched her walk down the hall with Blythe. She talked to José and not me. But why? She doesn't seem to be shy, and I was way nicer than José. But I guess she didn't know that. The worst part was when I thought about it I knew why she wouldn't talk to me. I am not so sure I'd talk to me at this point—fun facts or not.

Janie came up and hovered behind me. "'May the force be with you.' *Star Wars*, nineteen seventy-seven, starring Mr. Mark Hamill and Ms. Carrie Fisher." She leaned closer. I could feel her warm breath. "Sound familiar?"

I understood Janie right then. She can't stop saying movie lines, and I can't stop trying to talk to Abhi. We were compelled. That's the word Mr. Stankowitz kept using about protons and electrons.

I had to think of something to get through to Abhi. By now it was clear—even to me—that The Mission Distraction: San Antonio Fun Facts had been officially declared a disaster. What was I going to try next?

I knew I needed information, and I needed it now.

"Is Abhi from India?" I began interviewing Janie who still stood beside me.

"No," Janie said, rolling her eyes. "But almost. She's from Minneapolis."

"Okay," I nodded, memorizing the fact. Minneapolis.

We watched Abhi and Blythe disappear around the corner.

"Is she an only child like me?"

"No, she has a big brother in eighth grade who goes here." Janie shook her head. "Zack, you'd think you're the one who has trouble hearing."

"What are you talking. . . ?"

"Lesson one, Zack Delacruz," Janie interrupted. "If you want a woman to listen to you, listen to her first." And Janie stormed out of the interview so dramatically I could swear she had a cape trailing behind her.

I stood in the doorway wondering what makes Abhi so magnetic. And on top of that, why is Janie trying to help me? What's she up to? I mean, I was one confused kid. I don't even know Abhi. Well, I now know she's from Minneapolis and she has a brother who goes here. And she doesn't answer when I talk to her. My stomach gurgled.

Dazed, I stepped into the hall.

"Seek to get to class on time, Mr. Delacruz," Principal Akins said.

"Yes, sir."

But to tell you the truth, I was in no hurry to get to gym. After what had happened in the cafeteria, I cringed at the torture that was ahead. Gym is like the blacktop— too many students and only one Coach Ostraticki to watch over it. Okay, it's two if you count his tarantula mustache separately.

It felt like I walked toward a firing squad in a movie. The music started blaring loud in my head again, like a mariachi band at a Mexican restaurant on the River Walk. And everyone had plenty of insults to shoot at me: my khakis ripping and my Champ the Choo-Choo thong showing.

I felt my forehead, hoping for a fever, but no such luck.

The bell rang as I *swish-swish*ed into the gym, ready to run for the locker room and change into my gym clothes. I couldn't believe what I saw.

S tudents, still in their school clothes, were lined up against the left wall and the right wall of the gym, like a firing line.

Wha'? It couldn't be.

"Glad you could join us, Mr. Delacruz. It's a no dress out day," Coach O. said, his tarantula mustache dancing along. "We're choosing teams for dodgeball."

So it was a firing squad—middle school style. I hate dodgeball more than math homework, Brussels sprouts, or chin-ups.

Chewy Johnson emptied the red utility balls from a huge mesh bag. He lined up in the balls up in the middle of the shiny wooden floor.

Mom always says I am overdramatic. But seriously, dodgeball is like an old-fashioned execution. You stand in a lineup. Same. But instead of using bullets they shoot red utility balls, firing until you're out of the game instead of dead. Pretty much the same. In case you haven't figured it out, I am not very good at dodgeball. Let's just say I am an easy target.

"I was wondering UNDER-where you were!" José sang: "Champ the Choo-Choo *chones*." José touch counted each of his fingers. "That's 4C. I'm going to call you 4C for short, because you're already short."

While I gave José the "shut up!" face, Coach O. blew his whistle to quiet everybody down. I leaned against the gym wall.

José and Blythe were captains. Again. They were almost finished choosing teams. Abhi and Cliché were already on Blythe's team, leaning against the red mats that covered the gym wall. I tried to wave at Abhi, but before I got her attention, José pointed his finger at me, "Training pants, you're on my team."

I rolled my eyes and joined El Pollo Loco's side slowly, as if I were walking through chocolate pudding.

And then Blythe chose Janie because she was the last one.

"Yeah, baby!" Janie clapped her hands together like she was in it to win it. It didn't seem to bother her that she was a last-round draft pick.

When we played dodgeball, I was usually one of the first ones out, and today I was ready to be done with it all. *Take me down*, I thought to myself. But when I tried to jump in front of the firing balls, they'd miss me. When I tried to throw the ball so Cliché could catch it, I hit her in the shoulder instead. With her hand rubbing her shoulder she stared me down as she slid down the gym wall to sit with the other kids who were out.

"It was an accident."

Her scowl deepened.

She didn't seem to believe me. The weird thing was, the more I tried to lose, the better throws I made.

I became a red-utility-ball assassin.

"Play hard, 4C!" José yelled his support. At least it sounded like support.

And I played like a boss, dodging and throwing. *Boom!* I hit Blythe so hard her gold initial necklace swung up and nailed her on the forehead. My team laughed and patted me on the back, but Blythe looked at me like I had just stolen all the money from her student council pencil sales.

With all the cheers of support, a rush of confidence took control of my mouth: "Hate the player, not the game."

"You tell her, Champ," Sophia laughed. "But it's hate the game, not the playuh." Sophia smiled at me, turning to a scowl at Blythe, a not-so-subtle threat from our team.

I don't know where all the force was coming from— maybe it was science at work. Maybe there were positive electrons spinning around me. Whatever it was. I picked off Chewy Johnson, and he wasn't even playing. He was watching from the side. Then I nailed two other kids. I think I was beginning to like the power. I was dodgeballin'. Then Janie slammed one into Sophia.

"Out!" Coach Ostraticki yelled when Sophia didn't sit down.

My team was down to José and me.

Blythe's team had two, too: Janie and Abhi.

"Sorry, Janie," I mumbled. "This will hurt me more than it will hurt you." I hurled the red ball and smacked Janie's thigh with an audible slap, the ball bounced up and bashed into one of the caged lights high on the gym ceiling. She eyeballed me as she stomped toward the sidelines.

"I'll be back!" She stopped halfway to the wall. "*Terminator 1* and *2*, starring former governor of California, Arnold Schwarzenegger." And then she sat, giving me the *mal ojo*—the evil eye—the whole time.

"Ah! Ha! HA!" José taunted loudly.

"Soto!" Coach Ostraticki blew an exclamation mark with his whistle at José. "I'm gonna take you out of the game if you don't cut it out!"

Now Abhi was alone on the other team. Everyone on our team yelled. "Show her how we do it at Davy Crockett, Zack and El!"

"Yeah, give me a *T* and a *T* and a *T*! And a...!" Sophia yelled. "And another *T*. Go, go, go!" Sophia thrust imaginary pom-poms at us.

Coach Ostraticki tossed the ball to Abhi, so she could take the first shot. It was only fair.

José and I stood beside each other, waiting, rocking back and forth on our feet, ready to go this way or that to dodge the ball. Abhi threw the ball and it bounced right between José and me. Why I reached over and snatched that red ball, I'll never know. José didn't even try.

"Get her!" José roared, like he was avenging his father's death in a movie.

All my team stood up on the sidelines, yelling and

screaming. And all the shouting was getting to me. I thought about setting the ball on the gym floor and walking away.

But I didn't.

I stood and bounced the ball a few times, thinking.

"Are you a quitter, Zack?" José taunted me. "Are you man or thong?"

"Yeah, go Champ!" Sophia yelled.

The blue-eye-shadow gang shouted, "Yeah, go Champ!"

I bounced the ball again.

"What are you waiting for, Dela-*Loser*?" José taunted.

I raised the ball to my face.

And all the frustration and embarrassment from the day made my skin burn. Why did every terrible thing seem to always happen to me? My eyes were getting wet. I wasn't going to add crying to my fool portfolio. All my rage went into the red ball. I gripped it, not sure what to do. After all, I really didn't want to hit her. I wanted to talk to her. But if I threw the ball too softly, people would say I had a crush on Abhi. Then they would start heckling me from the sidelines. Just like this stupid game of dodgeball, there was no way to win middle school. So, I chucked the ball low and away, so I would just miss her leg. But at that moment, Abhi jumped.

The ball smashed into her ankle, and her legs flew back from the force of the ball. She slammed facedown on the hard wooden floor with a boom like thunder.

The gym went silent.

In the silence, I thought about how badly I wanted to explain to Abhi that it was an accident, a big misunderstanding. But nothing came out. I was just as shocked as everyone else.

Twice today I had made the loudest rooms in the whole school silent. And again, all eyes were on me. Maybe I needed to go back to fading into the cinder-block walls. This new, confident, out-there me was not working out the way I'd hoped. Like the sand crab in Mr. Stankowitz's aquarium, I wanted nothing more than to hide under a shell.

Blythe pulled Abhi to her feet. Coach Ostraticki approached her. Tears streamed down Abhi's face. Obviously they didn't have dodgeball in Minneapolis. At least they didn't have any *chone*-wearing-rotten-boys-who'd-throw-a-ball-so-hard-to-knock-her-off-her-feet kind.

I smacked my hand to my forehead: *Welcome to San Antonio, Abhi,* I thought. I'm Zack. I hope I gave you something else to remember me by.

"Next time take it easier on the new girl, Delacruz," Coach Ostraticki said, shaking his head, as if I had just shoved an old lady into oncoming traffic.

"You're a monster, Zack Delacruz!" Blythe screamed, hysterically.

I wanted to say I was sorry, but it all bottlenecked in my throat. I wondered if this was how it felt when you died.

"Balboa, that's not helping." Coach Ostraticki shook his head. He looked over Abhi, making sure she wasn't bleeding. "No broken bones, so she'll be okay."

Abhi nodded and started crying harder.

"Should we call an ambulance?" Blythe asked.

Coach Ostraticki ignored Blythe's question. "Balboa, when you can calm yourself down, please take Abhi to the girl's locker room to sit down and catch her breath."

José walked toward Abhi and Blythe.

"I never would've done that," José said to Abhi. "My dad insists I be a gentleman all times." He tossed his head over his shoulder toward me. "Sorry about Zack. He doesn't know how to treat a lady." He tapped his hand to his chest. "But I do."

That wasn't true at all. I was the one who knew how to treat ladies—I mean people. Nobody had to insist I act like a gentlemen because I already did.

Then it hit me like a dodgeball in the family jewels. Not today. Today, I took out the most interesting girl. Today, I slammed her face to the ground. Today, I made her cry. Today, I was that kid who won the dodgeball game for my team. But I wasn't enjoying it—not even for a second—because I knew I had lost any chance at getting Abhi to talk to me now. It was no victory for me.

Blythe began leading Abhi away to the girl's locker room, sneering at me as she passed, whispering, "Monster."

I stepped toward Abhi.

"Stay away from her!" Blythe turned and yelled. "Don't you think you've done enough?"

Coach O. blew two quick whistles. "Everybody, let's take two laps to remember how to be more sportsmanlike."

"That's just great, Zack," mumbled Cliché. "First Marquis is absent, and now this. I never should've gotten out of bed this morning."

It's official: my life was over.

~MMm~

I stood in the center of the gym, frozen.

Janie walked up beside me.

I sighed. "I just wanted to talk to Abhi, and now I've ruined it forever."

Janie nodded.

I looked up from the floor to Janie. "And I'm sorry I hit you so hard,"

"You hit everybody hard." Janie noted. "Let's get walking before Coach Ogre blows the whistle at us."

Janie's shoes squeaked on the gym floor as we rounded the corner. "Zack, I know something that would help you talk to Abhi for sure." Her words buzzed in the air like a swarm of gnats, daring me to swat at them.

I couldn't resist it. I was tapped out, obliterated, hopeless. What did I have to lose? "Okay, Janie. What can you do to help me fix this mess with Abhi?"

"I know things," Janie said.

I squinted.

"Mysterious things," she made her voice go all Halloween, echoey deep and low. Janie looked around to make sure nobody else could hear.

As if they'd want to.

"So what can you do?" I was desperate. Maybe I needed something mysterious or magical.

"My Aunt Monica is a *curandera*."

I stopped walking and looked at Janie. "She's a witch—a *bruja*?" I gasped.

"Noooo." Janie shook her head. "Not really. She's more like a doctor or a healer."

"How?"

"Like once she cured my brother Tito's cold by rubbing an uncracked egg all over his body."

"That's stupid. How's an egg going to help a cold?"

"It's science, Zack," Janie leaned in so close I could feel her hot breath as she whispered, "Magic science." Her fingers wiggled. "After Aunt Monica drew the sickness from Tito into the egg, she cracked it on a plate and placed it under the futon, so the egg could extract the rest of the illness."

"But I don't have a cold." I shrugged.

"So you don't need an egg. Besides, a dozen eggs wouldn't be enough for your case, Zack." She pointed at me. "What you need is something special from the *botanica*."

"Huh?"

"The *botanica*. It's a shop with a lot of herbs and oils and candles." Janie dramatically flashed both hands in front of her face. "Stuff with special powers."

"I've never heard of that."

"I know where it is because I've been there before with my Aunt Monica. Trust me, the *botanica* has just what you need, Zack."

"Why are you being so nice to me, Janie?" I asked.

"I already have to go to the *botanica* tomorrow after school anyway. I'm getting something for my Fall Fiesta-val booth."

"What does the *botanica* have to do with the Fall Fiesta-val?"

"Only Madame Bustamante knows," Janie's voice went deep and she rubbed her hands together. And then, like that, her voice went back to normal. "So are you coming or not?"

"I don't know, Janie."

"I do know." She closed her eyes and pressed two fingers to each side of her head. "Madame Bustamante is getting a vision. It's tomorrow . . . after school, and I see . . . yes, I see you, Zack Delacruz. And you're getting on the VIA bus with me." Janie shook her head as she came out of her vision. Opening her eyes, she pointed at José, who sprang up and down, trying to grab hold of the basketball net. "I'd come if I were you. He-who-jumps is already trying to impress the new girl."

"Janie, that's sounds—"

"Invite Marquis," she interrupted, "if you want."

That was all I needed to hear. Now the whole adventure sounded way less wacky. Marquis is like ranch dressing; he makes everything better. And I was ready to try anything after today.

The end of gym bell rang, which is also the end of school for me.

I *swish-swish*ed to the bus.

Abhi turned away when she saw me. She rides Blythe's bus—the one I take when I stay at Mom's every other week. I've only got a few days to fix this mess up. The festival is Saturday, and next week I have to take the same bus as Abhi and Blythe.

"Hey, T-Man," more than one person called out as I stepped onto the bus.

Great. Now I am the boy who wore a thong and knocks new girls off their feet—literally: zackdelaloser.com.

CHAPTER 8

I DON'T WANT TO TALK ABOUT IT

When I got off the bus, Mom's Honda was parked in front of the Villa De La Fontaine. What now? I wasn't going to Mom's house till Sunday. Did something happen to Dad? I ran to the car. I knocked on her window, panicked.

Mom opened her door. "Hey, Zack, those new pants sure look great on you."

"Mom . . ." I stood by her car, looking at the cracks in the sidewalk. "Why are you here?

"Can't a Mom come visit her baby bird?" Mom emerged from the car and closed the door.

I knew why she was really there. She wanted to have one of her talks. After the divorce, AD, Mom always sat on the edge of my bed and asked me to tell her what's going on. But that was at her house. She's never come to Dad's before.

And anyway, I couldn't tell her anything. If I did, I might let out Janie's plan for the *botanica*. Mom would never go for that. She barely let me take the bus to school. Mom's good to talk to because she knows a lot of stuff, but once you tell her something that worries her, she becomes a *Mom*ster.

"Aren't you going to invite me in?"

"I guess." I squinted up to the apartment, thinking about whether this was okay or not. She was my mom. But this wasn't really *her* apartment. Though it was mine.

"I brought a snack." Mom shook a plastic sack. "Almond butter and crackers." I love snacks. The offer of a snack wiped away any doubt I'd felt. Even if Mom only gets healthy crackers with seeds and stuff, I was sure it was be better than whatever Dad had in the pantry.

We walked up the steps. "How was the rest of your day, Zack?" Mom shot questions at me all the way up the stairs, like I was a suspect on some cop show and she was a tough detective.

"Fine," I lied. Plus, I couldn't tell Mom about today because she'd want to talk about every embarrassing detail, making me feel worse. BD—before the divorce—she never asked me about my feelings. AD—after the divorce—she never stops. I don't know what I'm feeling half the time, and the other half I don't want to tell my mother. I was careful not to give her any evidence she could use against me later.

"Oh . . . this is nice." Mom said, looking around the apartment. "Where do you keep your plates?"

I grabbed a paper plate from the plastic dispenser under the cabinet. Mom hates paper plates.

"Oh, how convenient." Mom spread the almond butter

on the "crackers," and questioned me about every last shred of the pants problem. I was so embarrassed.

"It's no big deal, Mom. I don't want to talk about it anymore." I knew I had to stop her before she asked me how I was feeling.

"Okay," Mom crunched her cracker. "But I'm your mom. Can't you talk to me about how you're feeling?"

I did the only thing I could: I crammed the last three almond butter-coated crackers in my mouth to buy time.

Mom continued. "I thought after today you might need to talk."

Chewing, I pointed to my full mouth. "*MMM-MMM.*"

Before she could grill me even more, Dad's keys jingled in the door. For the third time today everything went silent. Dad looked at Mom. Mom looked at Dad. I stopped chewing the dry ball of almond butter and cracker in my mouth.

"Carlos," Mom grabbed her purse. "Zack was just showing me the new place."

"Oh, well, I didn't know we were having company. I think we're still a few weeks away from really being settled."

"You'll have to have a housewarming party." Mom tossed the empty paper plate into the trash. "I know just what I'll get you." Mom started to wash the knife.

"I'll get that," Dad said.

"Sure." Mom turned and hugged me tight. "Hang in there."

After Mom left, Dad asked, "What was that all about?"

"Nothing," I lied. Sometimes things are just too

embarrassing to talk to your parents about. The good thing about Dad is, he only asks once, and then it's like nothing ever happened.

wwww

"Marquis?" I stretched out on the couch, gripping the phone with my shoulder.

"How's it going, Zack?"

"I don't even know where to start."

"Well, I am footloose and bandage free, so start wherever you want," Marquis snickered.

Without taking a breath, I told Marquis about the girl, the pants, the underwear, the dodgeball assassin, the magic shop, and the new nicknames. "Marquis, are you still there?"

"Yes," Marquis said, "But how can I be gone for only one afternoon, and all this goes down?"

He was right. Marquis usually kept me focused and calm, but with him gone today, I had really come undone like an old bent-up slinky. I needed his help to bend me back together. "Will you go to the *botanica* with Janie and me tomorrow?" I repeated *Please say yes* over and over in my head.

"What's a *botanica*?" Marquis asked.

"It's sort of like a magic shop."

"A magic shop?" Marquis's voice sounded more interested. "I can't see any harm in that. What exactly are we going to get there?"

"Janie didn't say really, but she said they'd have exactly what I need."

"And what is it you need?" Marquis's voice picked up speed and volume. "Some trick handcuffs or one of those never-ending scarves? Those are great."

"I don't know—something to fix this whole mess with Abhi. I really want to talk to her. I've got to figure out a way for her to see the real me, not the mean me she saw today."

"Now tell me again. Why do you want to talk to this new girl Abhi? I mean, what's the big deal?" Marquis waited. "And if you say it's her ice-gray eyes again, I'm hanging up."

I stared at the ceiling fan, spinning above me, rattling a little bit. "I don't know. I just do. Can you go with us? Please."

"I don't know if Ma will let me, Zack. But I am looking for a walking adventure to try out my new ankle."

"This will be an adventure for sure because I have no idea what I'm doing taking a bus with Janie Bustamante to some God-knows-where *botanica* magic shop. This whole thing has *adventure* written all over it."

"Let me talk to Ma."

"You could tell her we are going to the downtown library to do research. I mean, we are doing research in a way, right?" I laughed.

Marquis was not amused. "I don't know, Zack."

And to tell you the truth, neither did I. After we hung up, I rummaged around my room, the couch cushions, the drawers, anywhere till I'd collected all the change I could and put it with the five-dollar bill Mom had given me for raking up and bagging leaves last week. I even got out the silver dollars Grandpa had given me for my birthday. I popped them out of the plastic they were in, put the money in my backpack, and zipped it up.

I didn't know why I was trusting Janie Bustamante.

I guess I needed some magic on my side.

The next morning, Janie strolled into the cafeteria wearing a cheetah-print scarf wrapped around her head. Principal Akins made her take it off before she could get through the breakfast line, which is really just a trough of chocolate milk and Pop-Tarts. She grabbed a Pop-Tart, wrapped it in the scarf, and stomped out.

Marquis watched Janie exit the cafeteria. "I'm not so sure this adventure thing is a good idea."

"You're coming?" My face lit up. "For sure?"

He jingled the quarters in his pants pocket. "Got the bus money and everything. Even a few bucks in case I see a trick or something I want to get at the magic shop."

I grabbed his hand and shook it. "You da man, Marquis. What'd you tell Ma?"

"That I was hanging out with you after school to work on a project."

"Exactly," I said. "It's the truth. It's a magic project."

"I left the magic part out. She said I have to be ready to leave your apartment at six. She's picking me up."

"That's great. I'd have to be home by then anyway."

uwmm

Later, in Math class, Janie passed a note. When it arrived on my desk, ZACKVENTUROUS was printed across the front in bubble letters. Oh, my. I opened the note.

Dear Zack,
  I talked to Aunt Monica yesterday. She gave me all the directions, and I wrote them down. Bus #'s, and everything.
  After school, DON'T go to the bus circle. Go out the side door by the B gym. You'll have to figure out a way to get around Mrs. Darling. Then, we'll sneak out of the hole in the fence behind the baseball diamond. My big brother Tito told me all about it, and trust me, he knows more about escaping Davy Crockett Middle School than anyone else.
  See you after school on the other side of the fence.

  — Madame Bustamante

I wasn't really sure why she signed her name that way or why she was wearing that scarf on her head this morning. I've always thought Janie was one taco short of a combination platter, but this was getting me worried about the whole adventure.

"Hey, Zackventure or whoever you are," Marquis nudged me. "What'd she say?"

"We've got to go out the back of the school by the B gym."

"What?" Marquis's voice squeaked. "We can't go out the back doors! Remember what happened to El Pollo Loco last week? He got a day of In School Suspension for doing that." At Davy Crockett Middle School, to make sure all the students leave the same way at the same time, the teachers and administrators stand guard, forcing us get on a bus or leave from the front of the school. I guess they're pretty sick of kids by the end of the day.

"It'll be okay." I slid the note to Marquis.

Mr. Gonzalez, our math teacher, snapped his fingers, "Back to your problem-solving worksheet, gentlemen. Remember to show me how you solved the problems in three different ways."

Why wasn't one answer ever enough? Why isn't my life like this stupid math worksheet? I've got three problems for every solution instead of the other way around. I keep working on solutions all the time, but this time I only have one. This adventure to the *botanica* with Janie and Marquis had to work. Sorry, Mr. Gonzalez, there aren't three answers to this one.

wMMm

After math, in the hallway, Marquis confessed, "I don't even know what hole in the fence she's talking about."

"We'll find it." Now, I was the calm and centered one.

"I'm not so sure about this." Marquis played with the zipper on his powder-blue warm-up jacket. "I've never ridden on the city bus by myself."

"You won't be by yourself; you'll be with me—and Janie. Let's get to social studies before we get detention and never get out of this place."

As we walked down the hall, I thought about what he'd said. The VIA city bus was different. The school bus picked you up and dropped you off. On the city bus, you have to keep track of stops and change buses sometimes. Janie had better know what she's doing—especially now that I've dragged Marquis into this whole thing.

"It'll all work out. Trust me." I wasn't sure who needed convincing the most—Marquis or me.

wMMm

The rest of the day crawled by. But as PE ended, I felt a rush, knowing today we were skipping out on the regular bus—doing something secret. I told Dad I had to go to the library to work on a project, so I didn't have to be home till six, which should give us plenty of time. What parent could argue with going to the library?

In the hallway, Marquis and I took a right where we usually took a left.

Mrs. Darling stood watch at the side door by the B gym,

arms crossed, making sure no one sneaked out that way. I knew we had forgotten something. I had to think fast for a good reason for us to being going out the back door.

"Just be polite, while I think of something," I told Marquis. I had to come up with an excuse that Mrs. Darling would buy.

We walked up to Mrs. Darling.

"Good afternoon, Mrs. Darling." Marquis said.

"Hello, Zack and Marquis, to what do I owe the pleasure of your company on this fine afternoon?"

"Um . . . well you see . . . Marquis and I noticed some litter on the field," I said, "and we wanted to pick it up as part of . . . our service-learning project in social studies."

"Litter! It's the only part of *literature* I don't adore." Mrs. Darling laughed at her own bad pun.

I had to fight back a groan. *Be polite*, I repeated in my head, and I let out the fakest laugh ever.

Marquis looked at me, confused.

Mrs. Darling cleared her throat. "In any case, I love it when young people make haste to clean waste." Mrs. Darling smiled, peering around us. "Where's your receptacle for the litter?"

"Uh . . ." I looked to Marquis. "Ma'am I am not sure what you mean by *receptacle*?"

Mrs. Darling's face began to change into a question mark. "For the rubbish and refuse you find?"

"Mrs. Darling we're eleven—we don't know what those words mean."

"We're using my backpack . . . for the trash." Marquis interrupted.

"Oh, traaaash." I nodded. "Yeah, his backpack."

"OK then." Mrs. Darling stepped aside and flourished her hand toward the field. "Thank you for your service."

We forced ourselves to walk normally until the bell blasted. We turned and watched Mrs. Darling turn like a soldier and march back into the building.

I was the first one to bolt toward the baseball diamond that baked in the sun.

"Hey, slow down, man," Marquis huffed. "My ankle's not used to running!"

And for some reason, that cracked me up, and I snorted accidentally.

"Stop. I can't run. And. Laugh." Marquis panted.

Which was even funnier. This time Marquis snorted, and we both lost it as we rounded the baseball diamond. The field sloped down at an angle toward the fence that surrounded it. All the breaking up caused Marquis to slip. When he reached out to steady himself, he grabbed at me and then we both ended up tumbling down the hill, getting grass all over ourselves.

As we were lying at the bottom of the hill, my stomach clenched uncontrollably with laughter. I couldn't catch my breath. "Are you going to help me up?"

"Get yourself up, I'm searching for that hole in the fence Janie told us about." Marquis kneeled. "Here it is. I think." Marquis motioned to me. "Looks like more of tear than a hole." Someone had cut a straight line about as long as a skateboard through the silver chain-linked fence from the bottom up. Marquis grabbed the bottom of the cut and stretched the fence apart as far as he could.

"How are we supposed get through that?" I asked, still flat on my back.

"I don't know." Marquis studied the hole. "I guess we'll crawl through on our bellies. Are you ready?"

"Give me a second to catch my breath." I sat up.

A whistle blasted.

"Oh, no." Marquis looked over his shoulder. "Here comes the football team." Marquis hit the ground like a bomb was about to go off. "I knew we'd get caught."

CHAPTER 10
NO ACCOUNTING FOR TASTE

"Zack, what are we going to do?"

"Calm down, Marquis." I sat up and slipped my backpack straps off each shoulder. "We're going to get through this fence." I pushed my black backpack through the hole, careful not to snag it on jagged edges. The cut metal links were like sharks' teeth.

Marquis, still on his knees, grabbed both sides of the hole and spread them apart. I lay down right in front of the opening.

"Okay, here I go." I slithered through headfirst on my belly like some kind of middle school snake. The chain links kept catching on my shirt, and Marquis had to get them loose a few times, but I got through.

"Zack, we shouldn't have done this." He placed his hand on his belly. "My stomach hurts."

"We're almost there."

"But where's Janie?" Marquis looked at the hole and then back to the school. Hole. School. Hole. School.

"Your turn." I looked into Marquis's eyes through the chain link.

Marquis took a deep breath, zipped up his jacket, and slid his backpack though the opening. As Marquis's feet came through the hole, Janie came stomping down the hill.

I looked at Janie through the fence. "Janie, have you ever gotten through this hole before?"

"Nope." She slipped off her backpack. "Why?"

"Just curious." I looked at the hole and back at Janie.

"Pass me your bag," I said. I grabbed and pulled while Marquis held the fence apart. "Man, what have you got in this thing, Janie?"

"Supplies."

Marquis and I held the fence as far apart as we could. Janie went belly down and did this half inchworm, half ninja move through the hole in the fence. She moved like the star of a YouTube video.

She stood up and brushed the grass off her pants. "'My ninja skills are sweet.' *Big Hero 6*, two thousand fourteen."

Stunned, Marquis and I were speechless.

"Follow me." Janie walked to the curb.

Marquis and I looked at each other, shrugged, and followed.

"The first bus stop is up here on Valley Hi," Janie said, studying the directions on her white piece of paper.

We crossed the street to the bus stop. The sign looked like a metal lollipop on the end of a pole.

Marquis craned his neck to look up and down the street. Janie whipped out her map to study it again. I moved behind her, peering over her shoulder.

The map crinkled as Janie folded it closed, stuffing it in her front pocket. "I've got this, Zack!"

"I'm just . . ."

"*Ah tuh tuh tuh*," Janie shut me down. "I'm in charge of the directions."

"But—"

"*TUH!*" She jerked her shush finger up in front her mouth. "Don't speak! Marquis will watch for the bus, and you get the change ready: seventy-five cents each." She shoved some change in my hands. "And I am Madame Bustamante, the keeper of the map."

I dug into my pocket and pulled out some change. Marquis dropped his three quarters into my hand, one at a time. He never took his eyes off the street, as if the bus wouldn't come unless he pulled it to us with his eyes.

"Hold out your hands, boys," Janie ordered. She held a little red squeezy bottle with a yellow lid in her hand.

I don't know why, but I did what she asked.

"What's that?" Marquis winced, keeping his arms to his side.

"It's liquid candy—for energy." Janie squirted a line of it on the top of my hand, by my thumb and forefinger. It looked like line of bloody, wet sand.

"It's a spicy Mexican candy." Janie said. "It's *delicioso*. It says so on the label."

"Ma won't let me eat Mexican candy because she says she heard it has lead in it." Marquis shook his head.

I was finally getting a chance to try Mexican candy; this really was an adventure.

"Are you sure you don't wants some, Marquis?" Janie asked.

He didn't even answer. He was too busy looking up and down the street for the bus.

Janie showed me what to do. "Just lick it off your hand like this."

I licked the red candy scar off my hand. My eyes watered.

"Refreshing, isn't it?" Janie said.

"*Blahk!* No!" I reached in my backpack for the sports drink I put in this morning. I unscrewed the lid and swished the warm drink around in my mouth to get the candy flavor out.

"No accounting for taste," Janie shook her head.

"Here comes the bus! Here comes the bus!" Marquis sprang up and down, as if he had just won the *Price Is Right* Showcase Showdown.

I was glad the bus arrived before any of us could change his mind and head home.

T he quarters clanked as I dropped our fare into the slot by the bus entrance.

Janie sat and directed Marquis and me to sit behind her. Sitting sidesaddle, her arm rested on the back of the seat. "Now we've got a transfer to make, so make sure you pay attention. We have to get off at Commerce and Navarro, and then . . ." she looked at her map, "get on the 43 to South Flores."

"What?" Marquis leaned forward.

"Relax," Janie said. "I've got everything right here." She folded the directions and returned them to her pocket, patting them like she had a secret. I started to think I didn't like adventures.

As the bus pulled out, I was pressed into the back of the seat. I sipped my drink to calm myself.

"So, Janie, what are you doing at the Fall Fiesta-val anyway?" Marquis asked.

"I'm going to have a fortune-telling booth to raise money for the library." She smiled and leaned toward us. "Do you want me to tell you your fortunes?"

"How are you going to do that?" Marquis asked.

"I've been practicing for a while, but I'm buying a crystal ball today at Mama Lupita's, so then I'll be official."

"What's Mama Lupita's?" Marquis asked.

"Only the name of the best *botanica* in San Antonio." Janie noticed the confusion on Marquis's face. "Wait a minute." She looked at me. "Zack, did you tell Marquis anything?"

"Uh . . ."

"I thought we were going to a magic shop," Marquis turned toward me, puzzled. "You know card tricks and disappearing acts."

"Not exactly." Janie shrugged her shoulders, turning forward.

"You said it was a magic shop." Marquis slammed his hand on the seat.

"I said it was *like* a magic shop." I looked out the window. I knew I'd been careful to emphasize the word *like* every time I'd said it.

"To be fair to Zack, it is a shop that has magical stuff." Janie agreed, listing with her fingers. "Like magic candles and water and cologne."

"Magic cologne?" I tapped her shoulder. "What are you talking about?"

Now I was the one confused.

"Is that what you're dragging me across town for?" Marquis started poking me in the shoulder. "To get magic cologne for some kind of whackadoo voodoo?" Marquis's voice gets real high when he's upset; it was approaching a screech.

"Uh . . ."

"Oh, no, we're getting more than that." Janie shook her head. "Aunt Monica said we need a three-pronged approach: magic cologne, magic water, and a magic candle."

"That's casting spells. Not magic," Marquis insisted. "Magic is about tricks and slight of hand. Like Houdini."

"Marquis, maybe we need to get you some magic calming cologne," Janie offered. "And if you know about Houdini, then you know he and his wife were really curious about things like séances and crystal balls. It's a fact. I saw a Houdini movie the other night on the History Channel."

"No, ma'am. I am not going in that bo . . . bo . . . bo . . . tapioca place. No matter what you say." Marquis made the sign of the cross in front of his chest. "It sounds evil."

"Marquis . . ."

"Don't you 'Marquis' me."

"I'm sorry."

"It's too late for that." Marquis stood. "The only trick here is the one that was played on me." He moved to the seat on the other side of the bus, crossed his arms, and stared out the window.

Janie cupped her hand to the side at me. "We're already getting some attraction water, so don't worry about him." She put two fingers on each side of her forehead, doing the *Terminator* voice again. "He'll be back."

Before I could think of a way to get Marquis to move back to our seat, the bus ground to a halt. The doors opened, and riders got off and on. A bunch of tough guys with bandanas tied around their heads strutted on the bus. They all sat all around Marquis, smelling like BO and fists.

And just like that, Marquis sat next to me again.

Janie turned to us, pointing an index finger at each eye. "I told you I see the future."

The bus took off and pushed us back in our seats again.

Marquis glared at the back of Janie's seat, and I hugged my backpack to my chest.

CHAPTER 12
A SLICE OF DANGER

The transfer had been easy, but *ease* is not what I felt when the last bus pulled away, leaving us alone on a deserted sidewalk. Tall weeds poked through cracks in the cement. A chilling wind picked up, making the stalks scrape against us. Slowly, we looked around. With all the abandoned buildings, the street seemed like an end-of-the-world zombie movie.

"I don't think I've ever seen so many empty buildings in one place." I gulped. Graffiti covered almost every surface.

"No, sir." Marquis shook his head. I wondered if his stomach twisted like mine.

Janie pointed. "See that green building over there that looks like a slice of key lime pie?"

We nodded. The building—totally lime green from top to bottom—sat at a disturbing angle, a giant wedge of danger.

"The one with all the windows bricked in?" Marquis fidgeted with the zipper on his warm-up jacket.

"Yep," Janie said. "We're finally here."

On top of the slice of scary pie, a big painted white sign read "MAMA" LUPITA'S BOTANICA. For some reason *mama* was in quotation marks. Beneath that was a list: candles, perfumes, incense, powders, herbs, religious articles, and books.

"Why'd they have to brick in the windows?" Marquis pressed his lips together.

Ignoring Marquis's question, Janie spun around and marched ahead without us. But within seconds we'd caught up to her on the sidewalk in front of the store.

"I don't think Ma would be okay with this place." Marquis's voice quivered.

"Well," I whispered to Marquis, "right now being in *there* looks better than staying out *here*."

Marquis nodded.

But the feeling that the inside would be safer didn't last long.

Janie pulled the door open and a smell, like perfume spilled on a campfire, rushed out to greet us. We stepped in. I looked around the dimly lit shop. The walls, covered in pegboard, were like the cardboard brown ones in Grandpa's shed. Except at Mama Lupita's the pegboards were painted bright colors: red, pink, orange, and blue. And instead of tools, clear plastic bags full of dried-up leaves, tufts of fur, or metal charms hung on the *botanica* pegboards.

I turned to see a huge statue looming over me. Spooked, I stumbled back onto Marquis's foot.

"*Ack!*" Marquis yelped as if he'd seen a ghost.

"What's going on over there?" A woman snapped from across the store, her hair jet-black and her eyebrows pencil-thin. She looked old and young at the same time—ghostly.

"He was just was admiring your statue, Mama Lupita." Janie said, yanking my sleeve. "That's the Virgen de Guadalupe." Janie explained, making the sign of the cross in front of her chest.

"Wow, that statue is two-hundred and twenty dollars," I said. "She must be important." The statue stood watch over the shop and all the other Virgen de Guadalupe statues of various sizes all around the store.

"Why is she staring at us, Janie?" I whispered.

"She's a statue." Janie said. "Her eyes never move."

"Not the statue!" I whisper yelled. "Mama Lupita!" I pointed to the lady in black, who lifted her pointy chin.

Janie rolled her eyes and motioned me over to the cologne aisle. Each shelf was filled with small glass bottles, top to bottom, side by side, lined up like aspirin at a drugstore. Labels explained what the cologne would fix or do.

Across the store, Lady Doom still stared at us. Her thin eyebrows pinched, watching every move we made. She was seriously creeping me out.

Then—*poof*! Mama Lupita was standing beside us, like she'd been there the whole time. Marquis and I let out a gasp and grabbed on to each other.

"Hello," Janie said, unafraid, looking right into those black eyes.

"How'd she do that?" I whispered to Marquis.

First Mama Lupita was by the cash register and the next minute she's right beside us.

"My eyes are playing tricks on me." I nudged Marquis. "No way she could move that fast, could she?"

But Marquis just stared forward, clearing his throat. I focused on the shelves to take my thoughts off the magical shifting *bruja*.

I kept shopping and tried not to look afraid. Among the rows of small glass bottles, I saw break-up and attraction colognes. I turned to ask Janie a question, but the creepy lady was there instead. I flinched. Mama Lupita's arms were folded, revealing her black lace sleeves. Up close I noticed she smelled like an ashtray and had a tattoo of some thorny plant growing up her neck.

"Luck." Janie grabbed a blue-green cologne bottle from the top shelf as another Virgen statue watched us from the other aisle. "This ought to do it."

Mama Lupita grabbed the bottle from Janie. "I'll hold it at the register."

"WAIT!" Marquis interrupted, startling the rest of us.

The *bruja* stopped.

What now? I was freaked out enough without Marquis's shrill voice yelling every few minutes.

He thrust another tiny bottle toward me. "Here's one that says RAPIDO LUCK on the label." Marquis said. "I think Zack needs luck fast." He turned over the little bottle. The liquid was green but this one had a shamrock and a yellow horse on the label. "And look. It's two dollars and forty-seven cents, just like regular luck, so it's really a better value."

I cracked a smile. Marquis's bargain hunting calmed

him—and me too. Having Marquis act normal made me feel less nervous.

Mama Lupita put the unwanted basic-luck bottle back on the shelf, grabbed the new, better one from Marquis's hand, and walked back to the register.

Even Mama Lupita touching his hand didn't make him yelp this time. He relaxed a little bit and even smiled.

"I guess this place isn't so bad." Marquis admitted, crossing his arms. He leaned back a little too far into a coyote skin hanging on the wall, The skin dropped onto Marquis's head—the coyote snout and eyes landing face out, its legs framing the sides of Marquis's horrified face. *AHHHH!*" He shrieked and grabbed the coyote skin's paws, slamming it to the ground like a wrestler. He jumped up and down screaming and shaking out his hands.

"Don't make me throw you out. This isn't a playground!" Mama Lupita cawed from the cash register, burning a hole in Marquis with her charred black eyes.

Janie picked the coyote skin off the floor and gently hung it back on the wall. "Good boy!" She stroked it like it was her cat at home.

I turned back to Marquis and—*poof*—there the *bruja* was again, right beside us, smelling like cigarettes.

I mouthed, "How could she move that fast?" But then I realized I didn't really want to know—at all.

"I . . . I . . ." Marquis stammered, stepping away from the coyote skin, brushing loose hairs and evil off his back.

"It was an accident, ma'am." Janie assured Mama Lupita. That girl wasn't afraid of anything at all. In this store, easygoing Janie was the normal one. She rubbed her hands together. "Now for the candles. Do you have anything really, *really* powerful?" Janie asked her, as though she were in a department store inquiring where the shoe section was. "My friend really, *really* messed up with this girl he wants to talk to."

Mama Lupita smiled, revealing a set of really tiny baby teeth. I shuddered, holding back a scream.

"Which one?" Mama Lupita pointed at us. "The little jumpy one or the big jumpy one? Never mind, it doesn't even matter." She and Janie shared a smile.

Ugh! Those baby teeth looked like Tic Tacs poking out of chewed-up bubble gum.

Mama Lupita pointed. "Against the wall. Get him a candle. Powerful and impossible to mess up."

Janie practically skipped to the back wall. Relieved to leave Janie's new BFF, I followed.

"You know Janie, the cologne will be enough," Marquis said, trying to keep close, his hands in his armpits.

Mama Lupita's black eyes trailed us as we joined Janie at the wall of saint candles. From top to bottom, tall glass cylinders were plastered with saint stickers that explained what each candle cured.

"My *abuela* always lights these in her bedroom," I said, feeling better for a second. But Mama Lupita's had more than saint candles; they also had Luck and Fast Luck candles.

"Look, this one says if you burn it, you'll win the lottery." I held the candle out toward Janie and Marquis. "Does this work?"

"Aunt Monica says it will." Janie searched shelf after shelf, shopping for the right candle. "If you believe."

Marquis tilted his head, squinting. "If the candles actually worked like that, wouldn't everybody just spend the three dollars and ninety-seven cents and win the lottery all the time?"

"Be careful." Janie stopped searching for a moment. "If she hears you talking that way, she might put a curse on you." Janie tilted her head up toward the convex shoplifter mirror. In the distorted reflection, Mama Lupita stood behind us, scowling.

My pee alarm beeped in my head. I regretted drinking that whole sports drink. Actually, I regretted drinking any of it. I clenched and hoped it'd go away. Maybe I should look for some "no pee" potion. But first, I had to stop thinking about water—any water. But the more I tried not to think about water, the more water rushed through my mind like raging river flooding my bladder.

"You need this reversing candle." Janie handed me a tall red glass candle.

While Marquis paced, I read the label aloud: "Double-Acting Reversing Candle." I scrunched up my face. "What's this supposed to do exactly?"

"Just like it says on the label." Janie tapped on the glass. "It will double-reverse your bad luck."

"Something about *double-reverse* doesn't sound right." Marquis shook his head.

Curious, I dug my fingernail into the paper seal on the candle's top to see if it smelled like strawberry.

"Zack!" Marquis panicked, pointing at the handwritten

warning. A piece of white paper hanging on the shelf warned customers: "Don't poke holes in the tops of candles or you will be charged twice the marked price."

"Okay, okay, I won't poke the top." I said.

"Can't we go now?" Marquis pleaded. "Don't we have enough?"

"Two more things," Holding up two fingers, Janie moved ahead. "First, we need to get some attraction water."

"Please don't say that word." I didn't want to think about water.

"What word?"

"Oh, forget it." I stiffened.

Janie walked to the aisle and pulled a container about the size of a shampoo bottle off the metal shelf. It was filled with a red liquid. "'Attraction Water.' This will do it." Janie read the label as she moved down the aisle, "Can be used inside or outside." She was getting closer to the cash register. "You can even use it to wash your car."

By the cash register, Janie stopped in front of a locked glass display case. "Ma'am, I'd like the clear crystal ball, please."

The woman smiled at Janie, unlocked the cabinet, and removed the crystal ball. "This is what I've been saving up my money for." Grinning, Janie turned to us. "Isn't it beautiful?"

"I thought it'd be bigger," I said. The crystal ball was about the size of a softball. I looked down at the clear ball on the counter. I could see an upside-down image of Mama Lupita on the other side of the case, distorted as in the shoplifter mirror. But I could also see the three of us in it as I moved my head. What you saw moved as your head did.

"Twenty-three dollars?" Marquis asked.

"That's with the stand." Janie smiled, pulling a pink plastic coin purse from her backpack. "Plus my Aunt Monica is helping me a little because she's happy I'm following in her footsteps."

Mama Lupita started wrapping Janie's crystal ball. Finally, our shopping was done, but the sports drink pushed on my bladder like a water balloon about to burst.

"Janie, where's the restroom?"

"Ask her." Janie pointed to Mama Lupita, who still glared at me.

"I don't want to, Janie." I shook my head.

"Why?"

"I just don't." I looked to Marquis for help.

Silent, he shook his head no.

Janie looked at Marquis, then at me, and shook her head in a different way. Disappointed in what I guessed was our lack of adventurousness, she sighed. "I get it. I have to do everything." Then she threw her head back and laughed. "I kind of like it."

Marquis and I watched Super Janie go to work.

First she cleared her throat. Nice touch, but I hoped she'd hurry it along. Time was running out. "Excuse me, ma'am. Would it be a problem for my friend here to use your restroom?" She even batted her eyelashes. You have to give it to Janie. The way she said it was sweeter than the iced tea at Bill Miller's Bar-B-Que.

I stood there, doing the pee dance, moving my legs,

trying somehow to hold the sports drink in for just a bit longer.

Mama Lupita stared at me, said something in Spanish, and pointed to the sign: "No Restroom."

Gulp. When you're Hispanic and live in San Antonio, people expect you to know Spanish, but I don't really— just a few words here and there.

Janie interpreted, "She says there's a gas station a few blocks down that has a restroom."

Thing was, there was no chance I could hold it that long.

I sat my cologne, candle, and water on the glass case by the cash register and handed my money to Janie.

"Take my money, Janie. You pay for me." I made a beeline toward the door, calling back, "I gotta go!" I shoved open the door to the street, causing all the hanging bells to jingle and tinkle.

That tinkling sound was not what I needed.

"**W**hat's the matter?" Marquis asked, following me out the door. "There was definitely something weird about that place. Do you think that lady put a curse on us?"

"No," I jumped up and down on the sidewalk. "I just have to capital *P*, and I can't hold it."

"Well," Marquis offered, "that could be a curse."

The bells on the door clanged as Janie came out.

"Y'all turn around," I ordered, running toward the tall wooden fence at the back of the parking lot. The sports drink was in charge now, and it wanted out of me more than I wanted out of that store. How can a place have no restroom? My thoughts spun as I sprinted across the empty parking lot. I couldn't hold it for a second longer.

"Stay turned around!" I had to go so badly that my pee

made a loud thumping sound as it hit the wooden fence. I knew I shouldn't have done the capital *P* outside, but the sports drink wasn't asking, it was telling. Just another bad-luck disaster. I should've probably gulped down the whole bottle of Rapido Luck. But then I would have had to pee even more.

"I guess you did have to go," Marquis taunted from the other side of the parking lot.

"Shut up!" I yelled.

"Shuts don't go up. Prices do." Janie chanted from behind. "So take my advice and shut up too."

Janie and Marquis laughed, but I couldn't turn to yell at them because the stream wasn't ready to stop.

Behind me, the backdoor of Mama Lupita's flung open. The sound startled me. Without thinking, I turned to the side just as gust of wind kicked up and blew back a fine mist of the golden spray all over my khakis.

Mama Lupita shrieked something in Spanish.

I zipped up my pants and ran, trying to wipe them dry. I just wanted to get away from my bad luck, Mama Lupita, and the whole embarrassing situation.

"She's putting a curse on you, Zack!" Marquis screeched.

All I heard was *baño, malo*—or was it *mal ojo*?—and other howls that faded as we escaped. Those were three of the forty Spanish words I knew: *bathroom, bad,* and *eyes*. I heard those for sure. I think.

Together, we fled the scene of the stream.

"Let's get out of here before it's too late!" Marquis sprinted toward the bus stop across the street.

"But the bus isn't here yet!" I shouted. The wind

picked up and blew leaves around the street. I hoped it was also drying my pants. Janie and Marquis hadn't noticed the small damp spot yet, and it was becoming less noticeable by the second.

"The bus is the only way I know how to get us back to your apartment." Janie waved the directions in her hand.

"We have to get out of here before she casts another voodoo curse on us!" Marquis panted.

I wondered if Mama Lupita had cursed me. She couldn't, could she? Leaves swirled around my feet like the wind cursed us too.

I sped up.

"There's a church," Marquis yelled "We'll be safe in there."

But Janie passed the church, wheezing, the shopping bags clanking together. I had never seen Janie run in seven years of school. I didn't think I could panic any more, but if Janie was afraid enough to run, then I was terrified. *"Ruuuuun!"* I screamed to Marquis.

Marquis sped past me like a demon. You'd never know he'd gotten the bandage off his sprained ankle the day before.

After a block or so, Marquis bent over, panting. Janie and I stopped too. We stood in front of a yellow house surrounded by a white iron fence. The burglar bars on the windows matched. The breeze cooled the beads of sweat on my forehead.

I grabbed the top of one of the fence posts, catching my breath. "Hey," I gasped. "If we ever get home," I swallowed, "we should definitely try out for track."

Coughing, Janie sat on the curb.

"But what about the bus stop?" Marquis straightened.

Janie pulled out the directions. She carefully unfolded the sheet of paper. Just then, a gust of wind whipped up and ripped it from her hands. She reached for it, but the wind had whisked the paper straight up. I lunged off the curb, just missing it. Marquis hopped off the curb, waving his arms, but the directions somersaulted, higher and higher, higher than any of us could reach.

Tires screeched around the corner. We jumped back up on the curb in front of the yellow house and watched helplessly as the white paper with our directions floated above the street. As a red truck began to pass us, the air shifted. Then the paper suddenly dropped and landed in the bed of the truck.

"That's not even possible!" I yelled.

"It's the curse!" Marquis squealed.

"Hey, wait up, mister!" I yelled at the bad-luck truck. We raced into the street. Janie even did her two-fingered coach whistle. But the truck didn't stop.

"Zack, you need to get that Rapido Luck cologne out of your bag." Marquis shook his head, watching the truck and our directions disappear down the street.

"Oh, so now you believe." Janie placed her hand on her hip.

"I just believe we've got to get out of here. I believe none of us have a phone. I believe we're lost." Marquis pointed at me. "Zack's got a real curse on him, and it's spreading to all of us like a yellow fever!"

"Hey," I argued, "we don't even know for sure it was a curse." That's what I was trying to believe.

"Did you see what happened to our directions, Zack?" Marquis widened his eyes and threw his hands up.

"Yeah." I sighed. "I was there."

"How do you explain that then?" Marquis demanded. "How?"

I couldn't really. The truth of the bad-luck curse weighed on me.

Janie offered us each a piece of bubble gum, and the three of us shuffled down the street, directionless.

"What are we going to do?" Marquis asked, popping in a piece of gum.

"Give me a minute." Janie held up her hand, chewing her bubble gum slowly. "I'm thinking."

"Well," I said, "At least you got to test out your ankle, Marquis."

Marquis was not amused.

"We can be explorers like Lewis and Clark." I tried again.

"More like *Dumb and Dumber*," Marquis snapped.

Janie popped her gum. "If you say I'm Sacagawea, you're on your own, Clark."

A thunderous bark interrupted, making the three of us cringe. I almost choked on my gum.

We spun around. In an unfenced yard across the street, a white pit bull covered in black spots barked like we were on its dinner menu. Chained to a green, metal lawn chair, the pit bull raised its enormous head, barking and lunging toward us. He yanked at the chair, tipping it over on the ground. The pit bull charged, dragging the chair through the dry leaves behind it.

"Run!" I screeched. Marquis and I fled.

"No!' Janie shouted.

Whatever Janie said next, I didn't hear. I was already booking it as fast as I could. The scraping sound of the dog dragging the lawn chair mixed with my heart thudding, drowning out all other sounds. I looked back to see the pit bull run right past Janie, standing there with her arms folded.

"It's the curse!" Marquis shrieked. "It's possessed!"

"We can't stop!" I panted. Close behind, the enormous dog was gaining on us.

The pit bull closed in. But the chair snagged on a bush, slowing it down.

"This is our chance!" I said. We sprinted down the street. But soon the dog was right behind us again—along with the chair and a good chunk of the bush.

"I can't . . . run . . . anymore," Marquis sputtered.

I spotted an old black Camaro parked on the side of the street. "Marquis! Jump!" Both of us scurried over the hood and windshield like squirrels climbing up a tree.

The pit bull leapt at us. The dog's mouth was huge! It circled the car, bouncing around.

"It's getting ready for the kill, Zack." Marquis squeezed his eyes shut, folding himself up into a ball. I knew he was right. I'd seen predators circle their prey on the Discovery Channel. This wasn't how I thought I'd die.

"Pinky!" A lady's voice called from down the street. "Get over here, Shug. NOW!"

A lady with long red hair and freckles walked up. The dog, the chain, the chair, and the bush bounced and scraped over to the redheaded lady. She kneeled and Pinky practically licked the freckles off her face. She hugged the dog, then stood up and walked toward the Camaro, scowling: "What did you do to excite my dog so much? If you're going to play with her, play with her. Don't tease her."

Janie came up behind the lady. "We weren't teasing her, ma'am. My friends were scared, so they ran." There Janie was again. She could talk to anyone.

"But you never run from a dog. My Pinky is the sweetest, most friendly girl in the world!" The freckled, redheaded lady bent down and kissed Pinky on the mouth. Yuck.

Janie shook her head. "These boys don't know how to listen." Pinky trotted over to Janie, wagging her giant tail, the metal chair scraping in rhythm. As Janie bent down to pet Pinky, the dog immediately rolled over on her back for a belly rub.

I slid off the car. "Sorry, ma'am, I didn't know your dog was so friendly." I still wasn't sure, so I kept my distance. "Guys, we should go. It's starting to get late." I knew we had to get out of there before the owner of the car came out and skinned us alive for jumping all over his ride.

"Well, go on then," the redheaded lady said. "I hope you learned a lesson: If you run around in front of a dog, it thinks that you're playing." Pinky howled in agreement.

"Bye, Pinky." Janie scratched her ears. "Don't you want to pet her?" Janie asked.

"I'm good," I said, rocking my head from side to side. "We'd better go."

Marquis stood behind me. "Yeah, Zack's right, we need to go."

"Follow me," Janie said and off she went.

Marquis began walking ahead with his chest up, leaning back like his legs were pulling him forward, strutting like Raymond Montellongo and his eighth-grade friends.

"What are you doing?" I asked.

"I'm casually strolling like nothing is wrong." He

turned his head side to side. "I'm blending in. How do you do?" He turned his head the other way. "How do you do?" All the while strutting.

"Oh," I leaned my head back like Marquis, pushed my shoulders back, and strolled too.

"How do you do?" Marquis said and turned.

"Who are you talking to?" I asked.

"You just keep strolling like you own the street," Marquis said.

Janie turned back and shook her head.

"This is a good way to go." Janie looked around, her hand shading her eyes. The sun sets in the west." She would have made a good Sacagawea. "We're moving west, toward the setting sun," Janie said.

We looked up, shrugged, and followed.

Walking toward the sun seemed like a good idea at the time. That's the thing with the word *seem*. It's like *we'll see*. You know how when you ask if you can go to the mall to get a video game, and your mom says, "We'll see." Well, *seem* is kind of like that. It doesn't happen. Each block we walked, more things were in the yards: cars parked on the lawn, washing machines on the front porch, fast-food wrappers, cans, and toys everywhere. Things were all out of place—kind of like Marquis, Janie, and me

wMMm

After a while, we walked in the same rhythm. Three of us in a row, trying to hold in the panic. Marquis had been quiet for the last ten blocks. Yes, I counted. He hadn't uttered a word. That's zero words per block. Great. Now not only was I lost; I was applying math to my real life again. So depressing.

Since Marquis wasn't talking, the sounds in the neighborhood talked to me. Somebody blasted a stereo, the bass thumping like our steps on the pavement. Dogs barked. Block after block we got more lost, but none of us said a word.

"We are cursed for sure." Marquis spoke for the first time in almost eleven blocks. He stopped and rubbed the back of his neck.

"Just keep moving forward," Janie motioned us to follow. "We'll come to something soon. You have to believe." She walked toward the sun.

I started thinking we'd never get home alive.

All those stranger-danger warnings, all those Amber Alerts, and every movie villain I'd ever seen swirled through my brain, faster and faster. That's what I was starting to believe.

The three of us suddenly stopped walking all at once—we all saw the same thing.

CHAPTER 16

BUS TED OR CURSED?

"That's a bus stop!" Janie pointed half a block away, still leading the way.

That was the best-looking piece of metal I'd ever seen.

"But how do we know if it's the right bus?" Marquis asked.

"We'll ask the bus driver," Janie said. "I'll take care of it. The driver will know."

The sweet sounds of a bus grinding its gears caused us to yell in unison: "VIA!" Janie reached her arms forward as she ran. Now we were acting more like we felt inside: panicked. Once we climbed on the bus and found a seat near the front, we all sighed.

As the bus took off, we sat quietly for a minute.

I'd never been so glad to get on a bus as that one.

"Hey, sir," Janie said. "My friends and I are a little lost."

"My name's Ted, but my friends call me Bus Ted." He grinned in the rearview mirror, looking back at us, revealing his bucked teeth.

It was hard to hear him sometimes because he had to face forward to keep his eyes on the road, but at stops he'd turn around and tell us exactly what we needed to do to get back to the Villa De La Fountaine. Turns out Ted's ex-sister in law's cousin lived there. He gave us a shortcut to take home. Cursed people don't find helpful people like Bus Ted, do they?

By the time we made sure Janie got home, it was a few minutes after six o'clock. We were late, but we'd finally arrived at the Villa De La Fountaine.

"Marquis Monroe Malone, where have you been?" Ma, Marquis's grandma, yelled from the Lincoln's window. She cranked the ignition, and a puff of black smoke popped out, making Marquis jump. Without a word we waved good-bye, and I went inside the apartment as he climbed into Ma's Lincoln.

Because of Bus Ted's shortcut, we weren't late enough to cause suspicion. As I walked up the steps to 229, I decided the curse might not be real after all. How else would you explain us making it home? There couldn't be a curse. First, I bought everything from the *botanica* that Janie's Aunt Monica said I needed: the attraction water, the Rapido Luck cologne, and the Double-Acting Reversing candle. If I were cursed, I wouldn't have made it home with all of it. Right?

And after all the trouble we went through to get this magical stuff, I decided then and there that it had to work. I believed. Abhi would definitely talk to me now. My luck was going to change.

I opened the door to Dad's apartment and smelled grease and salt.

"I picked up some fried chicken."

"I'll be right there, Dad," I said. "I have to put my stuff down and go to the bathroom."

wWMvv

I didn't mention anything about Mama Lupita's to Dad—not the candle, the cologne, or the water. I worried he wouldn't understand. To tell you the truth, I didn't understand. But I had the magical water and candles. That's all I had to hold on to, so I had to believe it might work. Janie had said you have to believe. So I believed—or at least I tried to.

But I did ask Dad one question while we unpacked dinner.

"Dad, do you believe in curses?"

He pulled two paper plates from the dispenser under the cabinet. "Curses?"

"Yeah, you know." I popped the lid off the mashed potatoes. "Where somebody puts a curse on you."

"Like what?" Dad divided the bucket of chicken between our plates, dividing the drumsticks first.

"I don't know." I scooped up some mashed potatoes and plopped it onto our plates.

"What happened, Zack?"

85

"Nothing," I lied. "I just read about it in a book."

"Oh, okay." He tore into his drumstick. "I guess I don't really believe in curses that much." He pointed his drumstick at me. "But your *abuela* believes in a lot of stuff. She was always using her healing magic."

"She did?"

"You've seen the saint candles in her bedroom, right? That's a big tradition."

I nodded. "Why don't we have any?"

Dad shrugged. "And all the time when I was growing up, whenever anybody got sick, she'd rub an egg on you or something—or use this oil or special water." Dad licked his fingers.

"She did that?"

Dad nodded.

"Does that work?" I finished off my drumstick.

Dad wiped his hands on a paper towel and shrugged. "I don't really know. But I guess I always got better— eventually."

"Do you think you have to believe in a curse for it to work?"

"I suppose." He scooped up more potatoes.

"Then I don't believe in curses."

"Sounds good, my man." Dad headed for the couch with his plate, ending our *curse*-versation. "Want to watch a movie?"

"Sure." I brought my plate over to the couch and sat. That was the last that I mentioned curses and believing to Dad that night. But in my head I wondered about Abuela's eggs, oils, and waters. If she believed . . .

wwwww

After the movie, I scrounged up some matches and closed the door to my room. I repeated to myself over and over that I believed in the water; I believed in the cologne; I believed in the candle.

But not curses.

I unpacked the sack, setting out my three-pronged approach on the dresser. I lit the candle, splashed some attraction water on my face, dabbed some Rapido Luck on my wrists and neck, sat on the edge of my unmade bed, and waited for everything to change.

Before school the next morning, after my shower, I poured attraction water over my head. I almost made Dad and me late because I took so long air-drying in the bathroom.

"Stop stalling, Zack. Let's get a move on."

Still wet, I carefully slipped my clothes on. I topped myself off with some more Rapido Luck cologne and headed for the open door.

Driving out of the Villa De La Fountaine parking lot, Dad rolled the van window down. "Experimenting with cologne, my boy?"

"I guess." I opened the window too.

"Dad Lesson #203: With cologne, less is more."

"Huh?" I turned to Dad.

"Let's just say you put on too much."

"Okay." Staring forward at a smashed bug on the windshield, I felt embarrassment rising in my ears. Desperately, I licked my hand and tried to rub the smell off my arm.

"Son, that won't work." Dad motioned his head to dashboard in front of me. "There are some napkins in the glove box."

I opened the glove box, grabbed some loose napkins, and rubbed away. I was trying to *not* believe in curses. But it wasn't looking good for me at the moment. If you come to school with anything noticeably new—a new haircut, new glasses, you name it—you become a target for teasing. Too much smelly cologne will get noticed. Wiping my arm raw, I stopped, remembering I still wanted one person to notice.

"Hey," Dad said. "Look at me."

I turned and looked.

"It's fine. Really."

I wished I believed him. I turned up the radio and let the wind rush over my arm, hoping it would blow off the smell.

Dad lowered the radio. "Who is the cologne for?"

"It's not for anyone." I swallowed.

We pulled into the Davy Crockett Middle School traffic circle.

"Tell me about no one then." Dad shifted the van into park.

"Dad, I'm going to be late." I gazed toward the front doors as kids poured in. I grabbed the door handle. "Can we talk about it tonight?"

"All right." Dad sighed. "Tonight then." I opened the van door and slammed it. I joined the river of kids flowing into the front doors, hoping my Rapido Luck cologne had faded. But not too much. After all, I still wanted Abhi to talk to me. I disappeared into the hall.

But only for a second or two.

"Ugh! What's that smell?" Sophia yelled. "Who is that?"

Quickly, I ducked behind a large eighth-grader, hoping I'd disappear.

"I smell it too, Soph." Sophia's eighth-grade boyfriend, Raymond Montellongo, scrunched his face.

I peeked around my human shield to see if I could make a run for it.

"There he is!" Raymond strutted around to me. I tried to walk past him, but he kept blocking me. He leaned in and sniffed. "Oh, no! Shrimps played with his daddy's cologne."

The blue-eye-shadow gang held their noses. *"EWWWW!"*

José trotted up and started coughing. Then everybody coughed and grabbed their throats like I'd cut a wet burrito fart.

"Who is it?"

"It's Zack *Smella*cruz!" José pointed both fingers at me, like the guns of an assassin. He jumped up and down. "Smellacruz! Get it?"

"Man, Zack, you're supposed to dab on cologne, not bathe in it." Sophia shook her head.

I tried to get around the tower of Raymond: first on

his right, then on his left. But every time I moved, he moved, keeping me in the humiliation spotlight.

"*A-choo-ee!*" Cliché sneezed a tiny high-pitched sneeze. "I'm having a Zack attack."

"I need an oxygen tank," El Pollo Loco added.

Blythe pulled her blue cardigan over her nose. "Somebody open a window!"

The taunts and laughter and coughing closed in around me. I couldn't catch my breath. I spun around and sprinted into the bathroom. There, I rinsed my arms in the sink, tying to wash off the smell, wash off the stupidity of believing I could fix my bad-luck life. But the water only made it stronger. I grabbed for paper towels to dry my arms and neck.

Surprise.

There weren't any.

"Stupid curse!" I stared at myself in the mirror, dripping.

A trail of drops on the tile floor followed me to the cafeteria.

wWWm

"Do I smell Rapido Luck?" Marquis said, sniffing toward me.

"Don't even." I shook my head no, *n-o*.

We picked up our breakfast.

"With a strong hint of attraction water." Marquis smiled, nudging me with his elbow.

I stiffened. "The only thing it's attracting is attention— but not Abhi's." I snatched a chocolate milk.

"What do you mean?" Marquis asked, leaning over the milk cooler.

"Hey, Smellacruz!" A kid at the end of the line taunted. "Macy's called and they want you to return the truckload of cologne you stole." I didn't even know this guy.

"Oh, I see." Marquis nodded. "Well, look on the bright side. Now you know how much to put on next time."

I dropped my Pop-Tart and chocolate milk on the cafeteria table. "There isn't going to be a next time." I ripped open the foil wrapper of my Pop-Tart. "If this stuff is going to work, it had better start happening fast because I'm starting to think my whole life is an obstacle course."

"Or an obstacle *curse!*" Marquis smiled.

By now I'd lost my sense of humor, and if that wasn't a curse, then what was?

Marquis changed the subject. "Where's Abhi anyway?"

"She isn't in the cafeteria yet?"

"You mean curse-a-teria?" Marquis punned again.

I glared at him.

"Do you think this cologne-and-water stuff is going to work, Zack?" Marquis took a bite of his breakfast.

"I don't know . . ." I opened my milk. "Maybe. I mean, obviously people can smell me."

"*Uh tuh, tuh, tuh.*" Janie sat at our table for the first time. "It only works if you believe, Zack." Janie sipped her milk. "So believe it."

I nodded and chewed.

And hoped.

Janie pulled out her scarf and draped it over her nose.

In advisory, Abhi didn't talk to me.

In math, Abhi didn't talk to me.

In social studies, Abhi still didn't talk to me.

And just when I thought this *botanica* bath wasn't ever going to work, I heard a voice coming up behind me in the hall on the way to English.

"Belieeeeve, Zack."

I looked at Janie and sighed.

"Just give it time. Trust the cologne and water to do their work."

"It's only causing me problems so far," I said.

"When you truly believe in it, it will solve your problems, Zack." Janie and I walked into English. She stopped me and grabbed both of my shoulders, looking me in the eye. "'Hope is the only thing stronger than fear.' *The*

Hunger Games, two thousand twelve, starring my Peeta pal, Josh Hutcherson."

I nodded and sank into my chair, trying to believe a little longer.

"Stank you for staying on your side of the room," El Pollo Loco yelled. "Champ the Whew! Whew! What's that Smell?"

Mrs. Harrington started class by reading aloud "My Name" by Sandra Cisneros, who—fun fact—lives in San Antonio. I can't believe I ever thought fun facts about San Antonio could ever get Abhi to talk to me. Anyway, the story is about names and where they came from. While Mrs. Harrington read, the sentences took me away from my cursed day. I like how stories do that—take your mind on a trip for a while. The girl in the story was writing about her name—Esperanza—or "hope." I wished my name meant "hope," but I was starting to think it might mean "cursed."

After the story, Mrs. Harrington passed out a baby-name book to each table. "Have you ever wondered where your name came from?"

"I hope our parents, Miss," El Pollo Loco interrupted.

"Yes, José, of course your parents named you, but there could be a story about why they chose that name." Mrs. Harrington paused. "We can also explore the meaning behind your name. We call that your name's origin."

As soon as the baby-name book landed at our table, Marquis flipped it open and thumbed through it. "It says the *S* at the end of my name is silent. But I like pronouncing the *S* at the end of my name. Marquissssss." He whispered, deflating like a tire losing its air. "The other way my name sounds like Mar-kee."

"And that's the name of the sign in front of the school." I reached for the baby-name book. "Let me see."

"Wait." Marquis yanked the book back. "It says here it was 'a noble title derived from an Old French word *marches.*'" Marquis asked Mrs. Harrington. "Doesn't *noble* mean 'like a king'?"

"Well, it's like a high status," Mr. Harrington explained, "but not a king exactly."

"Yes, it says right here 'ruled the borderlands of the realm.'"

"What's a *realm*?" I asked.

"I don't know, but it sounds important." Marquis handed me the baby-name book. "I've got to look up *realm*, so I know what I'm the boss of." Marquis walked to the writing center and grabbed a dictionary.

I opened the baby-name book to the end. When your name starts with *Z* you are always at the end. Always. "It says *Zackary* means 'remembered by God.' It's a biblical name, so . . ."

"But I rule this realm." Marquis walked back. "The dictionary says I'm the boss."

"Did it really? Well, my name is biblical, so I'm like the king of kings." I shrugged. "Shouldn't I be over all realms?" Maybe going to church with Mom did have an upside.

"The gospel of Zack?" Marquis asked. We cracked up—it felt so good to laugh again.

"Ohhhh, I thought the name *Zack* meant 'smelly

dodgeball assassin.'" José looked over at Abhi, who was busy jotting something down in her writer's notebook. When will I learn to keep my big mouth shut?

"Or 'King Thong.'" José slapped his knee. "Get it?"

"All right, boys." Mrs. Harrington crossed the room to Abhi and Blythe's table. "Who else found out something interesting about their names?"

"I thought *Zack* was the name of a cheap cologne," Sophia whispered loud enough for me to hear.

"It's not even good enough for a dollar store,'" one of the blue-eye-shadow gang said. So now they were clever. Great.

At the table next to us, Abhi looked up from her writer's notebook and spoke softly. "My name means . . ."

Blythe held up her hand to tell Abhi to stop. "In a minute, Abhi. I think the student council representative for sixth grade should be next." Blythe stood up like she did every time she shared in class. I told you she was irritating. Pulling on the ends of her cardigan sleeves, clearing her throat, Blythe lectured us about her name.

"*Blythe* means 'happy.'" Blythe touched her *B* charm necklace and moved it up and down the chain. "I already knew that because my mom told me a long time ago, so officially I didn't even have to look it up." She did a mic drop of the book on the table, shooting a look at Mrs. Harrington.

"Thank you, Blythe, now I think . . ."

"Wait." She put her sweater stump up. "I am not finished. I can use it in a sentence."

"That's really not necessary, Blythe."

"I am *Blythe*—or happy—because my daddy said I'm going to drive the train he's building for the Fall Fiesta-val."

"I wish *Blythe* meant 'shut your cake hole!'" El Pollo Loco stood.

"José!" Mrs. Harrington snapped.

"Your dad is *not* going to let you drive a train." Sophia crinkled her forehead. "No way."

"Is to," Blythe glared. "Just wait and see, missy!"

"Okay," Mrs. Harrington interrupted. "What about you, José? What did you find out about your name?" I don't know what made Mrs. Harrington think calling on El Pollo Loco would get us back on track.

"Miss, I already know my name means 'the crazy chicken.'"

"I was hoping you'd find out the meaning of your actual name, José."

"Yeah?"

"*Abhijana* means 'of noble descent or royalty.'" Abhi announced, louder this time, standing like Blythe. But better, because she wasn't Blythe. She was Abhi.

"Ooh, she's royal like you, Mar-*kee*," Sophia said, not pronouncing Marquis's beloved *S*. "Maybe you should be in the same kingdom."

I cringed.

"Right?" The blue-eye-shadow gang ended her sentence, and the room got quiet, waiting for Marquis's reply.

Speechless, Marquis swallowed.

"Talk to the hand." Cliché held up her hand and stood between Abhi and Marquis. "*Cliché* is also French, just like

Marquis." She put her hand on her hip. "French means, 'I'm fancy.'"

"*Chewy* means *'knight'* with a *K*," Chewy stood, lumbering toward Marquis, excited to be knighted, his eyes sparkling through his bangs. "So I could work for you and Abhi, Marquis. I could guard your castle's moat." Chewy stood straighter.

Cliché continued, shooting Chewy a nasty glare. "French—as in 'Ooh, la, la!'" Cliché started reading from the word-origin book Mrs. Harrington had given her. "Platitude. Hackneyed phrase, commonplace, banality." Cliché realized nobody understood what she was saying— including her—and sat down.

"Make sure Chewy doesn't pee in your moat, Marquis and Abhi. Just sayin'." El Pollo Loco shrugged.

"José!" Mrs. Harrington changed the subject again. At least she tried. "Janie, what's your name mean?"

"I don't want to say." Janie said.

"Come on," Cliché encouraged. "Spill the beans."

"Yeah, Janie." Marquis smiled.

El Pollo Loco peeked over her shoulder. "*Dios mío. Janie* means 'God is gracious.'"

Everybody laughed, but I didn't. Janie slammed the book and put her head down.

"It's kind of like mine." I held up the baby-name book. "It's biblical." Janie lifted her head and held up her hand for a high five. Why not? I slapped her hand.

"Janie, shouldn't you be getting ready for your stupid fortune-telling booth?" Blythe snorted. "That's hysterical. Too bad I'm the only one whose daddy will let drive a train."

"Hold up." Sophia said. And just like that the whole mood changed. "You're telling fortunes, Janie?" She walked over to Janie, sounding sugary sweet. "I want my fortune told." Sophia was interested in what Janie could do for her.

"Well . . ." Blythe rolled her eyes. "I suppose that's okay, but you have to admit it's not driving a train, so . . ."

"Yeah, me too," El Pollo Loco said. "Read my palm, God Is Gracious." No one listened to Blythe anymore. All eyes were on Janie and her fortune-telling abilities.

Mrs. Harrington was too busy writing Chewy a bathroom pass to notice everyone gathering around Janie, circling her, not like sharks this time, but like fans who wanted her autograph. Man, middle school can change on a dime. One minute you're shark chum, and the next you're a celebrity everyone wants to be near.

Janie lifted up her head. "Really? You want me to tell your fortune?"

"Yeah," Sophia sat beside Janie. "I want to know about me and Raymond's future. And if I'm going to have a big hit song."

"I didn't know you sang." Janie looked at Sophia, pulling her hair behind her ear.

"Oh, I don't," Sophia said. "That's why I gotta know if I should start singing. Is it worth my time? If I'm not gonna have hit songs, why should I bother?"

I had to admit it—sometimes Sophia's logic fascinated me.

"Riiiight?" The blue-eye-shadow gang would be her background singers for sure.

"Yeah, and I want to know when a new pizza is coming into my life," José leaned his elbows on Janie's desk.

Janie laughed.

"You know you look good today, Janie," Cliché said.

"Yeah," Sophia nodded, "did you brush your hair or something?"

"No, I gave it a mayonnaise treatment last night." Janie touched her hair. "My Aunt Monica says it's a good conditioner."

"Okay," Cliché said. "Now you just made it weird." Cliché and Sophia got up, giggling as they returned to their seats.

"Save me a spot at your booth on Saturday, Janie." Sophia sat.

"Yeah, me too, Janie." Cliché sat.

Janie beamed.

"Your hair looks good, too," Cliché said to Sophia.

"I know. That's what everybody says," Sophia held her palms face up. "I use Miracle Whip." They cackled, closing the baby-name book on Janie for the rest of the class.

Why is it always like that? One minute you're almost cool, and then—*BOOM!* You're on the outside again. Everybody is just one mayonnaise treatment away from being an outsider.

I was about to ask Abhi about where her name came from, but before I could, class ended. And so did my believing in the *botanica* bath I'd given myself for no reason. I didn't need Janie to tell my fortune. I knew my future. And it didn't include talking to Abhi.

wwmn

After school, Marquis, Janie, and I stood in the courtyard, talking about how the attraction water hadn't worked like I wanted.

"Maybe when Abhi passes by, you could walk her to the bus, and the smell will overcome her." Marquis suggested.

"Yeah," I smiled, "I could ask her how she's adjusting to a new city and a new school."

"And," Janie added, "you have to give the attraction water another chance to work its magic."

Bzzz. Bzzz.

A few bees buzzed around my head.

"The bees think you're a flower." Marquis moved back. "It must be your attraction water." The bees kept coming, but they stayed away from Marquis and Janie. Maybe mayonnaise is a bee repellent.

Bzzz. Bzzz. Bzzz.

I swatted at them, jumping up and down, flapping my arms like I was crazy. At that moment, Abhi walked by, looking confused.

I stopped swatting. "Oh, it's not what it looks like, Abhi."

Abhi paused.

"Let me explain." I walked toward her as a bee stung my neck. "Ouch!" I slapped my neck, driving the stinger in deeper. "You stupid . . ."

Abhi flinched and hurried away.

"No, wait . . . I meant the bee, not you."

"Please don't hurt the bees," Janie pleaded. "They're so

cute and sweet that they go off and die after they sting you. It's their way of saying 'sorry.'"

I didn't have time to deal with Janie. I took off after Abhi and even more bees followed me like a cloud. "Nooo!" I yelled. Abhi turned around, saw me swinging at the air again like a madman, and this time she ran. Somehow I'd made everything even worse. I didn't think that was even possible.

Marquis walked up and stood a few feet away, out of the bee cloud. "Are you okay?"

"Just great. Now Abhi's afraid of me." I rubbed my neck.

"We'd better get to the bus," Marquis walked beside me at a safe distance.

"She probably thinks I'm crazy." I rolled my eyes at the bees surrounding me. "The bees are the only thing this attraction water does work on."

Marquis nodded, his eyes wide.

"Bye, Smellacruz!" El Pollo Loco yelled out of his bus window. "How you *bee*? To *bee* or not to *bee*, that's the question. Get it?"

Coach Ostraticki blew his whistle and the bees dispersed. I supposed they were afraid he'd make them run laps. Marquis and I climbed on the bus. "This stupid water and cologne caused me nothing but trouble."

I didn't say another word on the rest of the bus ride home. Marquis, being the good buddy that he is, allowed me this silent trip. I was done talking.

I knew what I had to do next.

wmmw

As soon as I walked in the apartment, I emptied the stupid *anti*-attraction cologne and the stupider *anti*-attraction water down the bathroom drain of the stupidest kid at Davy Crockett Middle School. My anger transformed me into the Incredible Hulk. I growled at my image and the mirror. I grabbed the Double-Acting Reversing candle and marched out to the Villa De La Fountaine parking lot. I hurled the candle into the Dumpster and listened to the glass shatter against the side.

I wiped the wetness away from my eyes with each wrist.

I didn't believe.

Not one bit.

None of it worked because it was cheap, smelly cologne, tap water, an ugly candle, and a wish. How could I ever believe any of that would change anything?

On the way to school Friday morning, I didn't say a word. Dad sure picked a bad day to make me ride the morning bus. Thanks, Dad. I waited for the insults to fly.

"What's the matter, Zack?" Marquis asked.

I crossed my arms tight and shrugged. "Everybody's going to make fun of me for yesterday."

"Nobody's said anything yet." Marquis looked around.

It was true. Everybody was too busy blabbing about the Fall Fiesta-val tomorrow. I wondered again if maybe the curse wasn't real. Maybe I should pay more attention to what's right than what's wrong. Maybe curses and attraction water weren't real, but I was. Maybe this is the day I finally get to talk with Abhi.

Cliché tapped Marquis's shoulder from across the aisle.

"Marquis, did you hear we're going to have to pay for the cascarones we made?"

"What?" Marquis's voice broke.

"That bossy, bossy Blythe Balboa forgot to mention that, after we made all those cascarones with our own blood, sweat, and tears, we'd have to pay for them if we want to smash them on our friends' heads." Cliché waited for Marquis's reaction.

He looked over at me.

"Maybe we should protest by not going to the festival," I interrupted.

"But it's a Fiesta-val." Cliché's mouth slackened.

"That's not fair." Marquis finally blurted it out.

Cliché looked at Marquis. "But we're still totally going," she almost demanded. "Aren't we, Marquis?"

Marquis nodded.

Great. I looked down at my feet.

Cliché turned around to the girls sitting behind her to plot a way to get cascarones for free.

"You have to come now." Marquis whispered, making sure no one could hear. "I need my wingman."

"What's a wingman?" I uncrossed my arms.

"I don't know. I heard it on TV. It's like your friend." Marquis looked around to make sure nobody could hear, and whispered. "My mouth gets all twisted up when I try to talk to Cliché. When you're there, I feel better."

I shrugged.

"So you're going, then?" Marquis nodded his head up and down, looking at me, waiting.

"Maybe." I stared at water droplets on the bus window.

"Cheer up, my man." Marquis spoke louder now. "Today is Friday. And tomorrow, we get to hang out together at the Fall Fiesta-val. There's a rubber-duck race and I hear there's going to be a dunk tank. Apparently no one has ever dunked Coach O. in the history of Davy Crockett Middle School festivals. Don't you want to try?" Marquis elbowed me.

"Yeah," Cliché joined our conversation, "We've got to at least try. We were the first sixth grade to be at the fall dance. We are the ones who can do it."

I looked at them both, grinning at me. "I guess."

"Well . . ." Marquis pointed his thumb to his chest. "I know." He winked at Cliché. Seriously.

I almost cracked a smile.

𝓌𝓂𝓂𝓃

On our way to the cafeteria, the three of us schemed about how we could dunk Coach Ostraticki and get free cascarones.

Marquis sniffed the air. I smelled it too: cinnamon rolls.

"It's cinnamon roll day." Marquis smiled. Good luck was in the air. Other kids noticed it too and walked faster. Some even ran toward the sweet treat in the cafeteria.

Everyone knows how I feel about the doughy, oozy, buttery, sugary goodness that is a cinnamon roll. Anyway, Davy Crockett Middle School only has cinnamon rolls once every two weeks. That's only twice a month—a mere eighteen times a year. Mr. Gonzalez, my math teacher, would be proud of my real-world math skills. Even math is better with cinnamon rolls.

Kids darted past us on our left and our right. Marquis looked at me. "Race ya!"

And he ran off. His ankle was stronger and faster than ever.

Cliché shrugged. "I'm not running. It's misting outside, and that courtyard will be slippery as ice."

To get to the cafeteria you had to go outside through a courtyard, which is really just a slab of concrete with a metal picnic table covered in bird poop.

"But it's cinnamon rolls," I said and took off.

The concrete outside the cafeteria was slippery. It wasn't my best idea to run, but since everybody else was racing to the cafeteria door, I did too. And besides, my luck was changing.

The bad thing was, if you slipped, no one would help you up. They'd trample you, leaving you covered with muddy footprints.

But worse, if you got in line after the cafeteria ran out of cinnamon rolls, it's cereal city for you. And once your nose has been teased by the smell of buttery, rich, sweet cinnamon sugar, a bowl of cold, soggy cereal feels like a nasty mush in your mouth.

My arms chugging, my mouth watering, I ran. Marquis, in the lead, ran inside the door. I decided to make my move and pulled ahead of Chewy Johnson before the cafeteria door swung shut. I wasn't going to be that guy stuck holding the door open while everybody else ran past.

"Oh, no!" The door slammed shut before I could make it through. I tried to stop, but my feet flew out from underneath me. I slipped, totally out of control, and I slammed right into the door that had just banged closed.

After the shock of hitting my head on the courtyard cement wore off, I looked up. And who had his hand on the door handle ready to pull it open and push me across the muddy cement?

That's right, El Pollo Loco. José gripped the handle and started tugging the door open, dragging me along with it.

A voice yelled out: "El, what are you doing to that little boy?"

Miraculously, José stopped pulling the door. He scowled down at me, but at least he wasn't dragging me across the muddy cement anymore.

"And let go of the door." The voice instructed.

José looked over his shoulder.

"NOW!" He let go of the handle.

Stunned, I searched through the mob that was yelling for me to get out of the way. I wanted to see who had such control over the uncontrolable José. My eyes came into focus on the person telling him off. To my surprise, it was Abhi. She stepped toward José. The other kids stood back. The powerful, most interesting girl was helping me—and not because I was flapping my arms like a crazy man. She was helping me like I mattered.

"Now, help him up," Abhi ordered José.

"Or what?' José glared back.

"Ooooooh!" The crowd's call to fight echoed off the cement courtyard.

Abhi paused. "You don't want to find out."

"Oooooooooooooh!"

Abhi had spunk. She just proved it's not always the boy

who saves the girl. Even though I was lying on the cement, cold and wet, I felt happy. My luck had changed. The curse might actually be broken.

Abhi sticking up for me felt pretty good. I mean, except for the part of me falling down and getting mud all over my shirt and khakis. And I guess Abhi calling me a little boy in front of a crowd wasn't my dream come true. And sure, it was just one more way I probably showed her I was a ridiculous shrimp who needed saving.

But she had noticed me—helped me, even.

José reached out his hand to pull me up. As I reached for it, he jerked it back just before I could grab it, teasing me.

"JOSÉ!" Abhi snapped.

"Okay, okay." José grabbed my hand and pulled me up.

"That's better." It's like Abhi was a trainer—a crazy chicken trainer. Maybe she could break José like a wild horse. Or tame him like a lion for a circus.

Abhi mussed José's hair, and his body relaxed like he was her floppy puppy dog. They giggled. As I tucked my shirt back in, I watched them as the crowds flowed through the door.

"Are you ready?" José asked, holding the door open for her.

"Yes, please." Abhi said. "I want to see these cinnamon rolls everybody's making such a big deal about. They must be spectacular."

They are, I thought, *like her*. What was that? I had this warm feeling in my stomach. All I know is that I wanted to talk with Abhi the way José did. As they entered the cafeteria, I brushed off my pants and followed.

From behind Abhi, I said "thank you," but she kept walking with José to the line, like she had never heard me. What was going on between the two of them? I wondered. Are they just friends or more? And what is *more*? And why is she with José and not with me? And was it too late? And would I still get a cinnamon roll? I came to my senses and got in line.

I got one of the last cinnamon rolls and caught up with Marquis. We ate side by side, watching José and Abhi laughing and eating.

José even gave her his last bite.

CHAPTER 20
DILUM AND GLOOM

L ater in line at lunchtime, Marquis and I each grabbed all they had left, salad.

"So what do you think is going on with Abhi and José?" I asked, sliding my tray down the track.

"Oh, man, I really wanted pizza." Marquis picked up his cardboard boat of salad. "I guess they talk to each other and they're friends."

"Friends like you and Cliché?" I asked.

"I guess because one's a boy and one's a girl." Marquis looked back at me. "Is that what you mean?"

"You know what I mean." I knocked my tray into his as we got to the cash register.

Marquis hung back to talk to Mrs. O'Shansky. "How's that garden of yours, Mrs. O'Shansky?"

I took advantage and squeezed a bunch of extra pumps of ranch dressing all over my salad.

"Fine and dandy, Mr. Malone," Mrs. O'Shansky said. "Just planted my pansies."

"Do tell," Marquis said.

I couldn't listen anymore. He wasn't even doing it for me to get extra salad dressing anymore. He enjoyed talking to adults.

I searched for a table in the loud cafeteria. That day, it was extra noisy and crowded because the eighth grade had an assembly and was eating early. I couldn't find a spot for two. I noticed someone following me. I turned, thinking it was Marquis.

It wasn't.

A big kid with eyes just like Abhi's towered over me too close. I backed up, but he kept coming at me. I had to bend my head all the way back to see his face. He looked me up and down, stroking his throat. "Hey, are you the little guy who took out my sister with a dodgeball?"

I searched for Marquis, who was still chatting with the Mrs. O'Shansky like they were BFFs.

"I'm Dilum Baht." He clipped the *T* at the end of his name. "What do you have to say for yourself?" He stepped closer.

"Nice to meet you?" I tried to calm him down. "Let me explain. I didn't do it on purpose." I sat my tray on the table and inched around to the other side.

Dilum followed, close.

"Then I didn't do this on purpose either."

Dilum made a fist.

I closed my eyes and held my hands in front of my face. "Please don't break my glasses."

Being polite, I guess, Dilum listened to my plea and slugged my shoulder instead. Hard.

"This is for my sister Abhi."

He hit me again in the same exact spot.

"This one's for everybody else."

Yowch! "What did I do to everyone else?"

Dilum poked my chest as he talked. "You shouldn't pick on people because they're different."

"Dilum, get yourself to an eighth-grade table. NOW!" Mrs. Gage, the cafeteria lunch monitor, bellowed. "This is no way to start at a new school." For once I was relieved to have Mrs. Gage all up in my business. She cut a beeline over to us. "We're not going to have a problem here, are we?" She looked back and forth at us.

I rubbed my arm and shook my head.

Dilum glared at her for a few seconds. Then, he threw his arms up and stomped to an eighth-grade table on the other side of the cafeteria.

Mrs. Gage let out a long sigh. "*Tsk, tsk, tsk.*" She shook her head.

Dilum kept pointing two fingers at his eyes to let me know he was watching.

"What was that all about?" Marquis sat across from me.

"I'm not sure." I rubbed my arm. "That was Abhi's brother, Dilum."

"Her brother is *that* giant?" Marquis opened his milk. "I bet this is all part of the curse that witch put on you at the botanical."

"*Botanica*," I corrected. "Curses only work if you believe in them." Though the way Dilum kept eyeing me, I had to wonder.

"I don't know. Maybe the curse is on me too." Marquis looked down at his pile of salad. "Did you notice how they ran out of pizza right before we got our trays?"

"Maybe we are cursed." I stared at the pile of lettuce I had drowned in creamy ranch dressing. Maybe I believed in the wrong things. "But there was plenty of ranch dressing. I got three pumps. Nobody was watching. You could get as much as you wanted."

"It's not pizza, though," Marquis interrupted.

It had gotten that bad: I was defending salad. I wished I could drown all my problems with creamy ranch dressing. But I don't think there was enough salad dressing in the whole world to cover all my problems.

"But you know, the whole dodgeball thing happened before the *bruja* put the curse on me." I poked at my soaked lettuce. "I mean, if she even did."

"Oh, are we talking about when you clobbered Abhi to the ground like a dodgeball assassin?"

"Um, you weren't even there." I squinted at him.

"People talk." Marquis grabbed a dressing-coated cucumber off my salad. "Are you going to eat this?"

"No."

Marquis crunched, wiping a drip of ranch off his chin. "That is a lot of dressing."

I pushed my soggy lettuce around, looking for a possible bite. "After Dilum hit me, he said something weird: 'You shouldn't pick on people because they're different.' What do you think he meant by that?"

"Well, maybe because Abhi's not from around here?"

"Oh, I didn't think of that." I shook my head. "But I never picked on her."

"Well, you did mow her down with a dodgeball." Marquis mumbled with his mouth full of lettuce. He swallowed. "That could've been seen as aggressive."

I sighed.

"And," Marquis continued, "you did look pretty upset yesterday with the bees and all your carrying on."

That stung.

"Did you ever apologize?"

"I tried to, but. . ."

"But what?" Marquis chomped as he waited for an answer.

"I don't have a reason." I shrugged. "I just never really got a chance."

"Well, you could start there." Marquis pointed his chocolate milk to the table across the room. "Go apologize."

Abhi sat at a table with none other than El Pollo Loco. The worst part was she appeared to be totally entertained by El, laughing and smiling.

"It won't help."

"You'll never know till you try."

I gulped down the rest of my milk. Marquis was right. I decided to apologize to Abhi quickly as I left the cafeteria—before Mrs. Gage or Dilum could stop me. Plus I could thank her for helping me this morning.

After I returned my tray, I watched Dilum. He was busy talking. I walked toward Abhi's table. When her eyes made contact with mine, she looked away—fast—like she was scared. Who could blame her? El Pollo Loco looked up when I arrived at the table.

"Well, if it isn't the Dodgeball Bomber. Did you swim through a cheap cologne ocean to get to school today?" He turned to Abhi, looking her in the eye. "I'll protect you, *mija*." He stood between Abhi and me, puffing out his chest.

My conscience hovered behind me: "Do what's right, Zack."

Actually, it was Janie again, pulling the strings.

"Does your girlfriend always tell you what to do, Zack?" El Pollo Loco taunted.

Mrs. Gage lumbered toward us.

"El, please stop." Abhi stopped smiling. "I was having fun talking with you. Don't ruin it."

That felt like a punch in the gut. But I had to say something fast before Mrs. Gage stopped me.

What could I say? Everything our school counselor, Dr. Cortez-Smith, had ever said about making friends and communicating flooded my mind: ask questions, find things in common, compliment.

José tried to stare me down.

I tried to ignore him.

"Looks like you *really* liked your salad, Abhi. You ate every bit." My mouth started chattering out of control.

What on earth was I saying? But I couldn't seem to stop. "Do you like to eat a lot? You seem like you do." I kept making it worse. "I didn't think vegetarians ate that much."

Abhi's gray eyes grew bigger and bigger.

"Fun fact, I'm actually . . . not . . . a veg—"

Janie slapped her hand on her forehead and walked off.

"All right, all right, Mr. Delacruz and Mr. Soto," Mrs. Gage interrupted. She called us by our adult names, hoping that would make us act like grown-ups.

"I'm not sure what his problem is, Miss." José sat back down. "Maybe you should send him to the nurse for diarrhea of the mouth."

"Enough!" From behind, Mrs. Gage placed her hands on both of my shoulders. "This is your second problem today, Mr. Delacruz. Let's try and show the new girl how respectful we are at Davy Crockett Middle School. Why don't you return all these trays?" She let go of my shoulders and turned to José. "Mr. Soto, please escort the young lady to the blacktop."

"But . . ." I tried to explain.

"Yeah, Zack," José jabbed. "When you're done, wipe down the tables." José held out his arm and Abhi linked her arm in his.

"No PDA," Mrs. Gage warned. That means "no public display of affection." It's in the student code of conduct.

Their arms dropped. El Pollo Loco swooped his charming bullfighter arm toward the door. "Ladies first."

Seething, I stormed over and returned their trays. Marquis came up behind me.

"I tried to apologize, but it . . ."

"I know, Zack. I saw everything. It wasn't your fault."
Marquis shrugged. "It's that curse."

"Yeah—and that's why I'm not going to the stupid fall festival tomorrow," I said.

"It's fiesta-val." Blythe interrupted, returning her tray. "Besides, you have to come, Zack. I'll be driving the train, and there will be cotton candy and hot dogs and who could forget *cascaRRRRones?*" Blythe rolled her *R*'s way too much.

Before Blythe went out the door, she turned and added, "And as sixth-grade student council representative, I order you to go." She held up her cardigan-covered hand like she was queen of Davy Crockett Middle School.

"See, Zack. You have to go," Marquis held back a laugh, putting his palms out. Marquis whispered, "Happy girl Blythe forgets this whole school is my realm. I'm the one who orders people around."

"Oh, yeah, Marquis." I sighed. "This whole thing's hilarious."

"All I know is you're going to the festival."

"Fiesta-v…" I stopped mid-correction. "I wouldn't be so sure."

As soon as we stepped onto the blacktop, everybody stopped to get a closer look at the fool of Davy Crockett Middle School: the fool who ripped off his pants in the lunchroom; the fool who blasted the new girl off her feet on her first day; the fool who stank up the school with cheap cologne; the fool who spazzed out in a bee cloud; the fool who slipped in the courtyard and had to be saved by the new girl.

Even so, I searched for Abhi on the blacktop for another chance to say I was sorry, to say thank-you for this morning. But once I saw she was with El, Sophia, and the blue-eye-shadow gang, I gave up. I'd never get to talk to her with them around. They would just talk about all the mud on my clothes or how I smelled up the school and every other dumb thing that I hoped Abhi would never remember.

Janie came up behind Marquis and me.

"Zack, I was practicing with my crystal ball last night. All I can say is . . ." she paused, "you need to go to the Fall Fiesta-val tomorrow. Your destiny awaits."

I sighed and crossed my arms.

Marquis lifted prayer hands to his chin, looking at me.

I uncrossed my arms and looked at Janie.

"I predict you will talk to Abhi at the Fall Fiesta-val. If you do not go, you might not ever have another chance to get to know her." She squinted and poked two fingers into both sides of her forehead. "I keep getting images of *cascarrrrrones*." She rolled her *R*'s just like Blythe. What is it with this school and stretching out letters?

"What about cascarones?" I asked. "Do I need to buy her some?"

Janie ignored me. "And a train." She opened her eyes. "But that's all I can see now. It's very fuzzy—the image isn't clear to Madame Bustamante yet."

"Oh." I held my palms out. I had a feeling why the images might be a little fuzzy. Part of me thought Janie's vision would go about as well as the cologne catastrophe and every other delusional disaster that had happened so far. But another part of me needed Janie's vision to be true, needed something to hang on to. And because I wanted to talk to Abhi, I had no choice but to believe there was something to her vision.

"Madame Bustamante and the crystal ball say it's your destiny, Zack. So . . ." Marquis gazed at me. "I can't argue with that."

Janie straightened her shoulders, raised her eyebrows, and stared at me.

"Okay, Okay." I hunched over. "I'll go to the stupid Fall Fiesta-val tomorrow. What have I got left to lose, anyway?"

"You could lose that curse," Marquis added.

"Marquis." I wouldn't look at either of them. "Be quiet before I change my mind."

The more I thought about it, the more I wondered if Janie really did know something.

CHAPTER 22
LET THE FIESTA-VAL BEGIN!

On Saturday morning, Mom dropped Marquis and me off in front of Davy Crockett Middle School. Her embarrassment mobile had huge real estate signs on the doors, so I always try to make a fast exit. At least Mom's car was less humiliating than Dad's orange Instant Lube van. But, trust me, it was a close contest.

Mom clicked the car in park and turned to us. "You two have a great time today. I wish I could go with you, but I've got houses to sell."

I grabbed the cold door handle. In San Antonio, it starts to get a little nippy in the mornings in November, but it warms up. I looked out the window and the sun was beaming.

"Aren't you forgetting something?" Mom asked.

"No," I looked at myself, checking. "I'm wearing my

hoodie." I patted my jeans pocket. "I've got my money."

"Are you sure there's nothing you need to say?"

"Bye?" I squinted.

Finally, from the backseat, Mom got what she was looking for. "Thank you for the ride, Ms. M." Marquis never forgets to say thank-you or call her *Ms.* instead of *Mrs.* and *M* instead of *D*. Mom liked him even more for using the right letter for her last name.

As Marquis and I piled out of the car, Sophia's mom honked her horn as she parked her van, yelling out her window, "Let's get our festival on!"

We waved. "That lady likes to have fun," I said.

"FIESTA-val, Mom!" Sophia slammed the van door. Everybody was out of uniform today. We can never wear jeans, so even Sophia wore them that day.

"Come see me at the cotton candy booth, kids!" Mrs. Segura waved. "That's my booth!"

Sophia walked away, putting her hair in a ponytail.

"Sure thing, Mrs. S." Marquis grinned. Man, he's good with adults, with people really. I could learn a lot from him.

The Fall Fiesta-val was held in the field behind the school, so we had to walk around the building through the grass to get to it.

Side by side, Marquis and I followed several clumps of kids. Sophia found Raymond, but from the murmur of the crowd you could tell a lot of people were at the festival already. Most of the kids we walked with were sixth-, seventh-, and eighth-graders from Davy Crockett. A few of them held hands with their little brothers and sisters.

And since this is middle school, nobody really wanted their parents there. The adults walked alone.

As we rounded the school, the excitement of the festival swirled through the crisp fall air. The sounds from the games mixed with carefree laughter. The smells of hot dogs, popcorn, cotton candy, and stomped-over grass invited us into the Fiesta-val. Over it all drifted the thrill of fun with friends and a freedom to do whatever we chose.

Mr. Akins's bullhorn boomed directions over the fun: "Fighting Alamos, please seek to form an orderly line for the required ticket-purchasing process. All events and foods must be acquired with tickets only."

"He can sure say a lot of words," Marquis observed.

"Yeah, but you must seek to use a Texas-sized dictionary to understand him." I sniffed the air. "It smells like a cookout at a swimming pool."

Marquis shaded his eyes from the morning sun with his hand. "I bet the dunking booth over there has chlorine in it."

"I can't believe the teachers are going to let us dunk them," I said, elbowing Marquis.

"Do I hear someone having a good time?" Marquis teased.

"Maybe." I pulled out a crisp five-dollar bill from my jeans. "Mom gave me some cash this morning. How many tickets will that get?"

"Twenty." *Math*-quis pointed to the handwritten sign taped to the ticket table. He pulled a gray duct-tape wallet out of his jeans.

"Since when do you have a wallet?" I asked.

"Since I became I man." He opened the duct-tape wallet and pulled out a few one-dollar bills.

"Oh, really." I smirked. "Since when do men get rides from their friend's mother?"

"The moment I made this wallet." Marquis shoved his wallet back in his pocket. "I found this on a YouTube channel. I'm a trendsetter. Duct tape is a fashion statement." He popped the collar of his black golf shirt and moved ahead in line. Marquis had a swagger about him, duct-tape wallet and all.

After we purchased our tickets, he patted my shoulder. "Come on, Zack. Let's roam."

A small train with red oil-barrel cars rode outside of the big rectangle of booths around the edges of the football field.

"There's Blythe's train," I said.

"And," Marquis smirked, "she's not driving, I notice."

Blythe waved from the caboose. "Everybody come ride the train. It's the only real ride here!"

"And it's slower than a snail." I watched the lawn-mower engine spurt some smelly black smoke, "I could walk faster than *that*."

"What do you want to do?" Marquis stopped and turned to me.

"Get cascarones!" I smiled.

"All right. But let's do the rubber-duck races first." Marquis rubbed his hands together. "I'm feeling lucky."

A little kid was holding his mom's hand and eating cotton candy. My mouth watered. "We are definitely getting some of that," I announced, nodding.

Music blared from the cakewalk booth. All these kids, young and old, walked around on these white circles with numbers on them.

"What's that?" I asked.

"They do cakewalks at Ma's church sometimes. See those cakes on that table over there." Marquis pointed to a long table covered with every kind of cake you could imagine. "When the music stops, they pick a number. And the person standing closest to that number wins a cake."

"Marquis!" Cliché yelled. "I'm going to win you a cake so we can share it."

Marquis waved back. "It's a date."

"Do you realize what you just said, Marquis?"

"It's an expression." Marquis scoffed. "C'mon"

"Maybe later I'll win a cake and give it to Abhi."

"Maybe you'll win a cake and give it to *me*. But that's later. Here's our first stop," Marquis pointed. "The rubber-duck race."

The booth had a painted sign with a huge yellow duck waving a black-and-white checkered racing flag.

After giving Mrs. Harrington our ticket, we waited for a PTA lady to give us a yellow rubber duck with a number painted on its back.

"Seven's my lucky number." Marquis raised his up, showing the top of his duck. "What did you get?"

"Let me dig deep for a good one for you." The PTA lady dug and dug in the bin all the way to the bottom and handed me a duck.

"Thirteen," I mumbled, my cheeks burned. "The most unlucky number possible," Maybe today wouldn't be a good day after all. Maybe bad luck did follow me around like a secret fart.

"Perhaps you shouldn't have thrown away that Double-Acting Reversing candle." Marquis teased, squeezing his duck, making it squeak.

I ignored him and plopped my duck in the water with everyone else's. The oval-shaped racetrack looked like a dug-out donut filled with water.

"How do we make our duck move?" I asked.

"You can splash with your hands all you want," Mrs. Harrington said. "But you can't touch the ducks, just the water."

Mrs. Harrington blew a whistle. "Whoever's duck goes all the way around the track first, crossing the starting line again, wins." She acted all teachery and looked each of us in the eye. "Remember, whatever you do, don't touch the ducks. You can only splash the water to move them forward. On your mark, get set, swim!"

"Go! Go!" We yelled at our ducks. Cramming our hands in behind the ducks, we splashed and pushed the cold water forward, moving the ducks on rolling waves and getting each other wet.

With all the splashing and yelling, I got into it.

"Come on, Thirteen!" I splashed. Everybody fought for space beside the track to splash their duck. Sometimes you'd move someone else's duck, or yours would go back.

Marquis nudged me, "See, thirteen doesn't have to be a bad number. We can't forget our country started with thirteen colonies."

We cracked up.

With everybody splashing and pushing, the water in the track sloshed from side to side. My eyes followed my duck as the hand splashes carried it forward. Thirteen was doing pretty well. *I might win this thing,* I thought. Duck thirteen got on the crest of a big wave, a huge swell, moving it ahead, faster and faster, up on a higher and higher bump of water, straight for the edge of the track.

"Not over the edge, ducky!" I yelled. But it was too late.

Unlucky Thirteen rode the crest of the wave right out of the track, crashing on the grass. The thirteen on its yellow back faced up, mocking me.

"Wow! That's never happened before in all the years I've run this booth." Mrs. Harrington looked confused. "Tough luck, Zack."

"I'm cursed," I mumbled.

"What?" Mrs. Harrington asked.

"Nothing." The crowd of kids continued cheering their ducks and splashing away. Of course, my duck was the only one who went overboard, an automatic disqualification.

Marquis's rubber duck took the lead. "Go Seven! Go Lucky Seven!" Marquis yelled.

I cupped my hands and cheered too. I still had a duck in this race!

Hands splashed wildly, and Marquis's duck crossed the finish line, winning by a beak.

"And the winner is rubber duck number seven," Mrs. Harrington announced, holding up Marquis's hand.

As we left the booth, Marquis showed me his prize—a tiny rubber duck reading a book. "I'm a lucky duck."

"Congratulations," I said. "Cascarones, next?"

"I don't know." Marquis crossed his arms. "That confetti and eggshell stuff gets stuck in my hair for weeks."

"Not everything is about your hair, Marquis."

"Well, almost everything *is*," Marquis sighed. "But I guess we can go there next."

"All right!" I smiled.

We searched for the cascarone booth,

A bunch of kids were carrying around fruit cups—a plastic cup filled with cantaloupe, watermelon, mango, and jicama with a squeeze of lime and a heavy sprinkle of chilé powder.

"We need to get one of those before we go too," I said. I was getting snacky.

"Do you want a fruit cup or a cascarone?"

"Cascarone."

Since we didn't find the cascarone booth right away, Marquis spotted Mr. Akins, wearing a black golf shirt the same as his. "I'll be right back."

He walked right up to Mr. Akins and started talking, probably about how they were dressed as twins. Marquis was like that. He wasn't afraid of anything—except cascarones in his hair and curses and coyote skins and *brujas*. I walked over and stood nearby so I could hear.

"At the present time," Mr. Akins was telling Marquis, "the cascarones booth is without a sponsor. It seems the sponsor had a cold-sore-related incident and is unable to distribute the cascarones. We are awaiting their imminent delivery."

"My friend here really wants to get some cascarones." Marquis pointed at me, standing there, looking like a goofball. I waved, awkwardly. "When do you think they'll be here?" Marquis asked.

"We're working on it at this very moment." Mr. Akins pointed to an empty table—no sign, no people, and most importantly, no cascarones. "I can tell you the booth will be right over there."

Disappointed, we started roaming the rectangle of booths again.

"Hey, if there are no cascarones like in Janie's vision," I wondered aloud, "will that mess up my chance to get to know Abhi?"

"Relax. Mr. Akins says they'll be imminently." Marquis stopped and pulled a few tickets out of his pocket. "Are you hungry?"

"Yep." Which was always my answer to that question. Is there any other response? Seriously.

"There's the cotton candy booth over there on the other side that crowd." Marquis waved the orange tickets. "My treat."

To get to the cotton candy booth, we passed through the huge mob of kids.

"What's going on here?" Marquis looked around as we snaked through half the population of Davy Crockett Middle School.

"They're filling up the dunking booth!" Chewy Johnson yelled over the rowdy crowd. "Mr. Stankowitz is up first—as soon as the tank is full."

Marquis and I stood on our toes to get a better view.

Holding a black hose, Manny the custodian stood on a ladder, filling the tank.

The booth was a dark-blue plastic container about the size of my grandpa's shed. It had this clear plastic on the front so you could see through to the water in the tank. It was only half full.

"It looks like a giant fish tank," Marquis said.

"They're going to need a lot more water." I nodded.

"Man, I've got to find a bathroom," Chewy said, turning to leave.

"Maybe you shouldn't watch the hose so close," José said to Chewy as they passed each other.

Where'd he come from?

"That clear plastic thing on the front lets you see the teachers swimming in circles like goldfish in a bowl after we DUNK THEM!" El Pollo Loco cheered and danced around in a circle.

Mr. Stankowitz inspected a little bench at the top. The sun glinted off his white arms as he stood perched high up on the dunking booth ladder.

Blinded, we all looked away.

"How's it work?" Marquis asked.

"See that stick coming out of the side of the dunking booth?" José pointed. "The target is on the end of it. If the ball hits it dead center on the red part—and hard enough— down goes Mr. Stankowitz."

"What will happen to those three strands of hair Mr. Stankowitz combs over the top of his head when he hits the water?" Marquis asked.

"Wait here and find out," El Pollo Loco said. "He's going up as soon as the tank is filled. Coach Ostraticki is after that."

"You know what would make this even better?"
Marquis turned to me.

"Cotton candy?"

"And a Coke." Marquis said, "We'll check back later."

It was a sugar 911. We hurried through the rest of the crowd to the cotton candy booth. As I followed close behind Marquis, I looked around for Janie's fortune-telling booth. I was still curious about her vision.

Marquis wove through the crowd, picking the path. I followed and kept looking around the festival. So I didn't even see Marquis stop. I accidentally plowed into him, knocking him forward into a big guy, who lost his footing and dropped his fruit cup.

"Somebody's gonna pay for this!" The big guy turned around, furious.

It was Dilum.

CHAPTER 23
FRUIT OF DILUM

"**Y**ou knocked my fruit cup on the ground, fool!" Dilum shouted at Marquis.

Oh, no! Now my bad luck was affecting my best friend. Quickly, I ducked behind a girl who had loads of teased-out hair and watched. The crowd backed up, making room for Dilum to fight Marquis.

"What's your problem?" Dilum towered over Marquis, covering him in his shadow.

"Nothing whatsoever. Dilum, right?" He stuck out his hand. "I'm Marquis. I know your sister Abhi."

Dilum slapped down Marquis's hand. "I don't care *who* you know or *who* you are. You don't shove me and get away with it."

The crowd started chanting, "Fight. Fight! FIGHT!"

Marquis gulped. "I can assure you I wasn't trying to

shove you. My friend and I are just trying to get to the cotton candy booth." Marquis looked around for me. I stuck out my hand from behind the teased-hair mound and waved.

"Well, isn't that nice?" Dilum started in. "It's going to be even harder to eat it with a sore jaw, you stupid klutz."

I'd never seen anybody so mad about a spilled fruit cup. And it was all my fault.

I had to do something fast. I had to save Marquis.

Marquis attempted to back away, but the crowd was too close for him to move. He was trapped. Dilum pulled back his hand.

I did the only thing I could think of. From behind the hair, I bellowed: "Are those the cascarones over there?"

The crowd stirred, pushing Dilum one way and Marquis another, turning back and forth, hunting for the cascarones that had finally arrived. Except they hadn't arrived. So people kept looking—everywhere.

Marquis and I fled to other side of the crowd—out of Dilum's view.

"You can't yell 'fire' in a crowd, but you can yell 'cascarone.'" I said. "There's no law against that."

"Let's just keep moving."

"Hey, look!" I said. "There's the cotton candy booth and there's no line."

Things were looking up. We escaped Dilum without a punch, a warm sugar smell filled the air, and there was no line at the cotton candy booth.

Marquis stared forward. "That was close."

I guided him to the booth. "I thought you were buying me cotton candy."

"That's all you want from me—my tickets." Marquis handed over the tickets, cracking a smile.

Mr. Gonzales, our math teacher, made Marquis's cotton candy first. He twirled a pointy paper towel roll thing in a big metal bowl on top of a machine.

My mouth watered. The pink glassy strings glistened in the sunlight as he handed Marquis the cotton candy.

"I'll make yours, Zack!" Sophia's mom nudged Mr. Gonzales to the side with her hip. She rolled the cardboard cone around in the cotton candy machine. Mrs. Segura didn't do it like Mr. Gonzales—at all.

"I'm new at this, *mijo*!" She apologized over and over as the cloud got bigger and bigger and bigger. After a few minutes she handed me a cotton candy the size of a human head. "I hope you like it."

"I do." I was in awe. "This is huge!"

Marquis looked at his. "No fair. Yours is twice as big."

And it was. It was an enormous pink cloud. My luck was changing, I thought, as the cottony sweetness melted on my tongue.

CHAPTER 24

WHO'S DRIVING THE TRAIN?

had plenty of my fluffy cloud of cotton candy left, but my stomach hurt. Marquis's was long gone. We strolled by the booths of hot dogs and sodas.

"I can't even think about food," I said.

The noon sun bore down, and little beads of sweat formed on my temples.

"You want the rest of this?" I held out what was left of my pink cloud.

As Marquis finished off the last bit, my eyes landed on a huge banner: DAVY CROCKETT TRAIN DEPOT. "Hey, look at that!" I elbowed Marquis.

"All aboard!" Blythe's dad wore blue-and-white pinstriped overalls and a train conductor hat. And Blythe was dressed as his twin. Except, of course, for the blue cardigan worn on top of her overalls.

"Come ride the train my dad made!" Blythe yelled. "Only two tickets. All profits go to the student council!"

"This could be a cool way to check out the whole festival," Marquis said.

"Fiesta-val," Blythe sneered. "Tickets?"

Marquis and I each handed Blythe two orange tickets.

As Marquis and I walked around the train, admiring it, people began loading onto the train cars, which were made from four red oil drums turned on their side. A seat hole was cut out of the top of each empty oil drum. I kneeled down and examined the four wheels that were on a two-by-four axle.

"Look at that engine," Marquis called me to the front of the train. "Is it a riding lawn mower?"

"Well, not anymore." Mr. Balboa beamed. The mower was black with shiny chrome mufflers poking out of the sides of the enormous engine. The monster tires were larger than the ones on a riding mower.

"This is awesome." Marquis reached out his hand toward the engine.

"Don't touch that." Mr. Balboa warned. "It's very hot."

"Did you make this yourself?" Marquis asked.

"I did." Mr. Balboa stood tall. "I work at the motorcycle shop and I added some new pistons and mufflers." He grabbed the bill of his conductor cap. "I calibrated the engine to go even faster than we'll go today."

"How fast can it go?" Marquis was in full-on interview mode, like he was writing an article for the school website.

"Faster than you'd think." With a red rag like dad uses at Instant Lube, Mr. Balboa polished a spot on the engine.

"On the weekends, I race riding lawn mowers."

"He almost won a couple of times." Blythe bragged.

"I will for sure with this one," He patted the seat of his suped-up mower. "She's got power! But talk is cheap."

We climbed in the last passenger car, right behind Blythe and straddle the beam, which ran down the middle of each oil drum. I sat in the front of the barrel and Marquis behind me.

After Blythe's dad climbed onto the engine and sat behind the wheel, I tapped Blythe's shoulder. "Hey, I thought you were going to be the driver. How come you're only taking tickets?"

Blythe spun around. "Daddy says I have to watch him a few more times before I can take the wheel."

"Yeah, and he also said talk is cheap," Marquis tapped the side of the barrel.

Blythe sneered. "Mark my words, Mister. I will drive." She spun around. "It's time to leave, Daddy." Blythe was a bossy assistant conductor too.

The mower belched smoke as Mr. Balboa pulled the throttle on the side of the engine.

One of the first things we passed was Janie's fortune-telling booth. I figured Mr. Akins had approved her wild-cheetah-print scarf, because she was wearing it—on her head. The gold jacket she wore glowed in the sun. I squinted. It looked like it had flashing red lights attached to it. That couldn't be. I needed a closer look.

"Janie!" Marquis cupped his hand and yelled from the seat behind me.

In the middle of her crystal ball reading, Janie threw

her hands in the air, stood, and whirled around, her gold jacket twirled around too, almost floating like a queen's robe. "It's Madame Bustamante!" She bellowed. She bowed to nonexistent applause and sat back down.

"Get that? Madame Bustamante, not Janie," I turned to Marquis. "She told you!"

"And that's all she's telling me today."

"You're not going to her booth with me?" I whined.

"No sir. I've had enough magic. Today, I am cotton candy full and magic free." He burped to punctuate his sentence.

The train drove around the outside of the whole festival in a big circle.

We passed the silly-string station, the strength-o-meter, and the balloon darts.

"I want to try my hand at the toss-a-rubber-chicken-in-a-bucket booth." Marquis patted me on the shoulders from behind. "I am on a winning streak."

Just then, the oil-drum train passed the rubber-duck races, where my losing streak began today. "I think I need to cut my losses. No more games for me. It's a waste of tickets."

"So you are going to see Ja—I mean Madame Bustamante—instead?"

"Yes, I am. But let's meet at the dunking booth when we're done. I want to see if Coach Ostraticki is going for a swim in his track suit."

"Sure thing, Zack."

Just then, we rounded the corner by the dunk tank. Things had already started with Mr. Stankowitz. The train stopped to let a group of kids pass.

We were just in time to see the ball hit the target with a BOOM!

Splash!

In went Mr. Stankowitz. He rolled around in the water like he was being attacked by a shark. José was twirling around laughing.

After Mr. Stankowitz stopped flailing, one of the strands from the top of his head stuck right between his eyes like seaweed on a diver.

"Well, now we know what happens to his comb-over when it gets wet." Marquis nudged me.

Raymond was the next person in line to dunk Mr. Stankowitz.

Mr. Stankowitz locked the bench into place but had some trouble climbing back up on it. His Davy Crockett T-shirt stuck to him like tight bike shorts.

"I'll never be able to un-see that!" El Pollo Loco yelled, shaking his head, running away from the dunking booth fast.

"Get him, Raymond!" Sophia yelled. "He gave me a bad progress report last week."

"Looks like she hired a hit man to dunk Mr. Stankowitz," Marquis said. We turned in our train seat to look back.

Everybody cheered Raymond on. He wound up his arm like he was pitching in the World Series.

The crowd rumbled.

Mr. Stankowitz shivered and seemed to hug himself, the strands of hair all sticking to his face. I felt sorry for him.

"Get him again!" Sophia screamed.

"Awww!" The passengers complained when the train started moving again at the best part.

Raymond let the ball go and it catapulted to the target, hitting square in the center.

BOOM!

Splash!

Down went Mr. Stankowitz again.

"Have you had enough?" Sophia yelled, knocking on the clear plastic of the tank.

As we got out of range of the dunking booth, I turned to Marquis. "Wow! Looks like the dunking booth's going to be pretty exciting."

Mr. Balboa interrupted, blowing a foghorn as the train came back to the station. José had started following the train and was catching up as it slowed down to stop. "Hey, kid, stop running with the train! We're coming into the station."

El Pollo Loco ran along the side of the mower, trying to talk to Mr. Balboa. "Can you make it go any faster?"

"Running next to the train is strictly prohibited!" Mr. Akins shouted into the crackling bullhorn.

Mr. Balboa blew the foghorn so close to El Pollo Loco's head that José finally stopped running and grabbed both his ears.

"*Ay!*" El Pollo Loco shouted and rolled around on the grass. "That hurt, Mr. Blythe's Dad!"

As we climbed off of the train, I overheard Blythe begging, sweet as cotton candy. "Daddy, you said I could drive. Pretty please." Her voice dropped lower as if she were going to feed him a poison apple. "Besides, I already told everybody."

Mr. Balboa nodded. Man, she was bossy: b-o-s-s-y.

"I'm off to conquer rubber chickens." Marquis headed off to the other end of the fiesta-val, waving.

"I'm off to conquer . . . something," I said. To tell you the truth, I didn't really want to split up with Marquis, but if there was any chance at all that the crystal ball could help, I had to at least try.

Out of nowhere José grabbed my arm—startling me. "How was the train ride, Zack?"

"Bouncy." I shrugged.

"All right!" El Pollo Loco leapt up and down, clapping his hands. "Is it fast?"

"It felt fast to me."

"Want to ride again?" He asked.

"With you?" I was confused.

"Yeah, come on." José begged.

"I can't."

"Why not?"

My mouth opened, but nothing came out. Why was El Pollo Loco treating me like a friend all of a sudden?

"I need somebody to ride with me." He bounced like a pogo stick. "Come ooooooon!"

"I'm on my way to get my fortune told." I pointed toward Janie's booth.

"Oh, wow!" José spoke fast. "Janie's fortune-telling booth—or I should say Madame Bustamante's fortune-telling booth—is so awesome! I went before the dunking tank opened."

"Really?" I was surprised to hear El Pollo Loco say something nice about Janie.

"She's got this real crystal ball and she's dressed in this shiny coat that sparkles and she uses this deep voice to tell your future. Get this." José looked around. "She predicted I would have many slices of pizza in my life very soon, and as soon as I walked out of her booth, guess what I found on the ground?"

"Pizza?"

"No, better. I found some tickets on the ground."

"Oh," I said, nodding.

José leaned in. "And guess what I bought with the tickets?"

"Pizza?"

"Exactly." José pointed his finger at me. "She's like a for-real fortune-teller and everything. Everybody says she tells you something true."

It wasn't exactly a miracle that she'd predicted José would be eating pizza soon. But finding the tickets on the ground right after he left the booth—that was pretty cool, I had to admit. And it was miracle he talked to me like I was a human being. That was a good sign.

"Well, laters." José handed two tickets to Blythe's dad and climbed into the last train car. "I'M THE CABOOOOOOSE!" José screamed, shaking his caboose as well as the train's as he boarded.

"Enjoy the ride, José," I said. You have to say this for El Pollo Loco: he really enjoys himself.

He waved back from the train, grinning.

I turned and walked toward Janie's booth, wondering

if Janie really could predict the future. Did she really have a vision? Did I have any better ideas?

The answer to the last question was a definite no, so I trudged toward Janie's fortune-telling booth, hoping.

CHAPTER 25

NOT A FORTUNE FOR YOUR FORTUNE

A black posterboard with white chalk letters was taped to Janie's fortune-telling booth: *"Not a Fortune for Your Fortune* by Madame Bustamante" was written in fancy letters. Two tickets for your fortune. I dug in my pocket, and I pulled out exactly one piece of lint and two orange tickets. Was it a coincidence or fate?

I got in line behind Cliché, who was next, so I'd make it to the dunking booth on time. I counted six people waiting in line.

"Madame Bustamante" sat behind a long table covered in a brown paisley bedsheet. Her hands floated above the crystal ball from Mama Lupita's, which lay in between Janie and her client.

Beneath the cheetah-print scarf swirled around her

head, Janie wore a headband made of an old bike chain spray-painted gold.

I squinted to see Madame Bustamante's hoop earrings. They looked like she'd cut them off the end of cardboard paper towel roll. At least I hoped it was a paper towel roll and not a toilet paper one.

Mrs. Darling caught me staring at Janie. "Madame Bustamante's costume is perfectly divine, is it not?"

Mrs. Darling's book-shaped earrings gleamed in the noon sun. But they were nothing compared to the blinding glow of Janie's gold overcoat. It had pointy shoulders and was covered with red glistening jewels sewn all over like chicken pox. Watching her jacket shimmer in the sun was worth the price of two tickets alone.

Mrs. Darling cupped her hand, like she was telling me a secret. "You know, that jacket Janie's wearing is from the Mrs. Darling collection. I am quite handy with a sewing machine and gold lamé, don't you think? I only wear it for special occasions."

"Oh, do you tell fortunes too?" I asked. If she were a fortune-teller, it might explain a lot about her wardrobe.

"Why no, my dear." She adjusted her fluorescent orange poncho. "Janie is helping me raise funds for the library." Then Mrs. Darling struck a pose, tossed her scarf around her neck, and like a circus ringleader announced, "The one and only Madame Bustamante!"

I dropped the tickets and the piece of lint in Mrs. Darling's hand.

"Thank you for your support as always, Mr. Delacruz." She picked out the lint, letting it drop to the grass.

As soon as Mrs. Darling skittered away, Cliché turned to me. "What are you here for, Zack?"

"Answers."

"Same here." Cliché crossed her arms as if she were giving herself a hug. "I hope Janie can tell me if I'll be able to date Marquis in eighth grade."

"Why eighth grade?"

"Because that's how long my mom said I had to wait to have a boyfriend."

I nodded.

She sighed and watched the festivities.

The roar of the lawn-mower–oil-drum train rattled the fortune-telling booth as it passed. It was definitely going faster than when we rode it.

"Blythe's driving the train!" Cliché gasped, putting her hand to her chest.

"What?" I whipped my head around. I couldn't see over the people in the next booth, so I stood on my toes, squinting. It was true. Blythe was behind the wheel in her conductor hat and sweater, driving the train solo.

"I can't believe it! Her dad's not even with her." Cliché put her hands on her hips. "No fair! I bet he'll let that Bossy Blythe have a boyfriend in sixth grade too."

"Huh?" I tilted my head.

"Never mind."

Blythe waved her sweater stump as she rode by.

Jealous, Cliché and I smiled through gritted teeth, waving backwards like we were in her realm.

Chewy Johnson yelled as he passed. "Let me off this crazy thing." I guess the train didn't take bathroom breaks.

147

"Blythe was telling the truth the whole time," I said.

"I know." Cliché shook her head. "I never believed her when she rattled on and on about it."

"I bet it'd be fun to do something you're not supposed to do yet." I watched the train circle around the festival.

"Like what?" Cliché asked.

"I don't know," I stammered. "Like drive a train, I guess."

"Or do something your mom tells you not to." Cliché got a faraway look in her eyes.

"Huh?" I twisted up my face.

"Oh, nothing." Cliché reached down and fidgeted with her little white lace socks. "This is all Blythe will talk about for the rest of the year."

"I know, right?" I gasped. Oh, no! Things were taking an ugly turn: I was starting to sound like the blue-eye-shadow gang.

"Zack, what are you going to get Janie to predict?"

I looked down at the worn grass beneath my feet. "It's personal."

"Well, excuse me, Zack." Cliché turned away. "I thought we were friends."

"You did?" My jaw dropped.

"Um, I was talking to you, wasn't I?" Cliché didn't turn back around.

C liché had a point.

She had been talking to me. I stared at the back of Cliché's pigtails. One barrette was purple, the other pink. I wondered if she had worn two different barrettes on purpose.

I'm like Cliché's barrettes in a way, I thought.

I'm two different Zacks: one who does stupid things and the other who does great things. One who believes in bad luck and one who believes in good luck. And probably, nothing I'll ever do will change how people see me. Some people might pay more attention to the purple, but the pink is still there, always.

"Cliché," Mrs. Darling interrupted my wondering mind, "would you be a dear and collect the tickets for the fortune-telling booth?" Mrs. Darling put her hand on her head as if she had a splitting headache. "It seems the parent in charge of the cascarrrone booth (she rolled her *R*'s too much like Blythe) is dropping them off in the parking lot and can't come in for medical reasons."

"That's super important!" I said way too loud. "I was afraid the cascarones might not make it."

"Never fear, Mrs. Darling is here." She handed the white zipper bag of collected tickets to Cliché.

"Okay." Cliché took the bag. "Then, can I get my fortune for free?"

"I'll pretend I didn't hear that, Cliché, because you know this is raising money for our library." Mrs. Darling said over her shoulder as she raced off to pick up the cascarones. "For the good of the many!"

I stood in line behind Cliché, thinking about Abhi and luck and how I really needed to know what Janie had to say about it all. The festival would be ending soon, and I was running out of time.

"It's about Abhi." I mumbled to Cliché's shoulder.

"What?" Cliché turned back.

"It's about . . ." I looked up. "Abhi."

"What's about Abhi?"

"The fortune," I said.

"What do you need a fortune about Abhi for?" She rubbed her arms and tilted her head.

"I want to get to know her."

"Why?"

That was a really good question. "I don't know really." I shrugged. "I just do. Plus, I need to apologize."

"For the dodgeball incident?"

"Um, yeah." Why did everyone call it an incident? An accident, yes. An incident, no. "And I also have to thank her for the cinnamon roll day incident." I had to admit the word *incident* does come in handy.

"You like her, don't you?" Cliché broke through my racing thoughts.

"I just want to talk to her." I said. "Every time I try to talk to her she acts like she doesn't even hear me."

"Yeah, Zack." Cliché's voice changed. "That happens when someone can't hear very well."

"What?" My face scrunched up.

"Remember she told us on her first day you need to look her in the eye when you're talking to her." Cliché leaned in.

"Abhi?"

"Who are we talking about, Zack?" Cliché threw up her hands.

"What do you mean Abhi can't hear very well?" Now I leaned in, interested.

"On her first day here, in science class with Mr. Stankowitz." She crossed her arms. "Oh my God, Zack! You don't know how to listen."

I turned away. Cliché sounded like Mom scolding me.

"Just pay attention to what happens in front of your face, and your life will be much easier."

Okay, Mom must have paid her to say that.

"You really have no idea, do you?" Cliché asked, realizing I was serious.

"I guess I wasn't in the room yet or something," I put my hand up. "I came in late."

"You were too in the room," Cliché bobbed her head as if she were a talk show guest and I her brother who pawned her Barbie collection for video game money.

"Sometimes I get all up in my head thinking about stuff and I sort of zone out."

"You missed a lot, Zack." Cliché said. "For example, Blythe blabbed to everyone that Abhi wears a hearing aid."

"But I've never seen one." My eyes widened.

"Duh, she doesn't want you to." Cliché said.

"How come nobody else said anything to me?" I scowled.

"Because anybody who listened could tell Blabber Mouth Blythe had embarrassed Abhi." Cliché got all Mom-like again. "How would you like it if everybody talked about how short you are?"

"But they do." I shrugged.

"Then you should understand more than anyone else. She didn't want to be the girl with a hearing problem." Cliché sat in a chair and folded her arms, resting her case like a lawyer on TV. "She just wants to be treated like everyone else."

I remembered that Marquis hadn't been in Mr. Stankowitz's class that day either. He was at the doctor. "Marquis doesn't know either."

"So what? Why are you making such a big deal about all this?" Cliché turned and collected two tickets from a kid who got in line. "No wonder she doesn't want anyone to know. This is what she didn't want: everybody talking about her hearing problem instead of who she is as a person."

"Next!" Janie bellowed in low voice. How'd she make her voice go that low?

"Here, take this." Cliché handed me the white bag of tickets. "It's my turn."

I clutched the ticket bag and looked out across the Fall Fiesta-val. Marquis threw a rubber chicken toward a line of mop buckets. I searched for Abhi too. Maybe all those times she just didn't hear me.

Maybe I didn't listen.

And maybe all I had to do was look her in the eyes and tell the truth.

At that moment my eyes landed on the most interesting girl—Abhi, all by herself on the field, eating cotton candy. I waved, but she didn't see me.

This was my chance.

I should leave the line.

Except I was next.

And I was the ticket taker.

But maybe I didn't need my fortune told. Maybe it's like attraction water and Rapido Luck cologne. They never worked.

Or did they?

The attraction water worked a little bit on Cliché. And José. They usually aren't that nice to me, but today they were. Really nice. If that's not good luck, what is? Cliché even called me a friend. And she gave me advice—like a friend.

Pay attention to what's going on in front of you. Cliché's voice tumbled though my head, getting louder and louder.

I decided then to start paying more attention to what was in front of me instead of what was going on in my head.

And it was a good thing I did, because I couldn't believe what I saw next.

CHAPTER 27
SERIOUSLY, HOW FAST IS THAT TRAIN SUPPOSED TO GO?

T he train raced by the booth again. Why was it going
so fast?

"Something's wrong," I said to no one in particular.

The train rumbled along, going way faster than before.
Blythe yanked at her sweater sleeve, which seemed to be
caught on the side of the riding mower engine

"It's stuck on the throttle thingie!" Blythe pulled and
pulled her too-long sweater sleeve, stretching it out, longer
and longer. The more she pulled, the faster the engine roared.

"Stop pulling on the throttle, Honey!" Mr. Balboa
yelled, trying to catch up to the runaway train.

"But my sweater's caught," Bossy Blythe wasn't going
to listen when her beloved cardigan was at stake.

The terrified passengers let out a long scream as they
rounded the corner, tipping to the side and landing upright.

Blythe gripped the steering wheel of the racing mower, yanking and pulling at her sweater sleeve, rocking her shoulders from side to side, almost losing her balance a few times.

"Please!" Mr. Balboa panted. "Just take off your sweater!" He leapt for the riding mower, just missing it. Instead, he knocked over the fishbowl game table, lined with twenty glass bowls that people were tossing ping-pong balls into to win a goldfish. Water and ping-pong balls and shattering fishbowls spilled to the ground. Mr. Balboa landed on top, apologizing as he tried to get up, slipping on wet ping-pong balls.

"What's going on here?" Mrs. Gage, who was in charge of the fishbowl game, stood over Blythe's dad as if she were going to give him lunch detention.

A few parents jogged alongside the train.

Blythe gave one last jerk to her sweater as the train passed the cotton candy booth and started to head around again. The sleeve finally ripped free, wrenching off the speed lever. The suped-up mower roared, now thundering at top speed. The lever dragged and bounced and clanked on the ground along with Blythe's stretched-out sweater sleeve, which got longer and longer as it unraveled. Somehow the sweater was still connected to Blythe.

"Take off your sweater, Blythe!" Her father yelled, pulling a goldfish from the neck of his shirt.

"But it's my absolute favorite!" Blythe screamed back, gripping the wheel with both hands. The unraveling sweater pulled her to the side.

"Do it now, Blythe!"

She took her hands off the wheel just long enough to roll her sweater off her shoulder. The sweater swept under the train and exploded into a puff of blue shreds.

The final yank burst the mower into a full-on Harley sound: *rrrrrumm gggrrrrrrrrrrrrrumm neeuurrrrm!* The train was more like a motorcycle on the highway than a passenger train at a school fair. Mr. Balboa wasn't exaggerating about his riding mower having the speed to win races.

Mr. Akins jogged to catch up to the train. "Ms. Balboa—*squeaaaaal*—please seek to slow down that train at this very instant!" he yelled into his white bullhorn.

"I CAN'T!" Blythe screeched.

From the back car of the train, El Pollo Loco, the only passenger enjoying the runaway ride, held his hands up in the air. "Look, Ma, no hands."

Moms and dads and teachers stood, frozen like me, not knowing what to do. Most of the kids were at the dunking booth, cheering so loudly to dunk Coach Ostraticki, they had no idea about the out-of-control train careening around the festival borders.

Out of the corner of my eye, coming from the parking lot, I saw what looked like a pizza deliveryman with a giant stack of pizzas. But when I saw the hot pink sandals moving along the ground beneath them, I knew it was actually Mrs. Darling, and the pizzas weren't pizzas at all. They were the cascarones! The way she wobbled made me think she needed a hand. I looked at the train, I looked at the cascarones, I looked at the dunking booth. I looked back at the train. I wasn't sure what to pay attention to.

Then, Abhi caught my attention again. She smiled, looking so happy. And for one second I forgot all about Blythe Balboaconstrictor's oil-barrel train disaster and Mrs. Darling, the human cascarone tower.

Suddenly the train passengers screamed a roller-coaster scream, jolting me back. Blythe had swerved to avoid the duck-pond races and Mrs. Harrington. That turn put her on a straight path for Abhi. And the worst part was, Abhi couldn't see what was coming up behind her, fast.

Just like the dunking booth crowd around her, Abhi watched, hoping the tormentor of our days, Coach Ostraticki, would get dunked. Yelling, screaming, laughing, and facing the wrong direction, none of them saw the train coming.

"*Studens!*" Mr. Akins bellowed through his bullhorn, still trying to catch up to the train. "Please seek to remain calm."

Abhi tore away pink cotton candy fuzz and ate it, watching the excitement at the dunking tank, oblivious to the disaster headed straight for her.

CHAPTER 28
THE BEST RIDE EVER

"Out of my way! Out of my way!" Blythe shrieked as the train bounced across the field at breakneck speed.

Hearing the commotion approaching, Abhi turned, but froze.

I threw the ticket bag to Cliché, interrupting her fortune telling.

"Hey!" Janie and Cliché shouted.

"I've got to save Abhi!"

Janie stood. "Zack, you will. I can see it clearly now. 'This is your destiny. Never look back, Darling. It distracts from the now!'"

I sprinted toward Abhi, yelling, "*The Incredibles*, two thousand four!" as my battle cry.

The train careened right for her.

I pumped my arms as fast as I could.

The train growled and spit black smoke from its shiny mufflers.

"MOOOOOVE!" Blythe shrieked.

The lawn-mower train was twenty feet from plowing Abhi down, flattening her like a vegetarian pancake.

"Disperse, *studens!*" Mr. Akins screeched into his bullhorn. "Seek to disperse!"

"Remember the Alamos!!!" El Pollo Loco hollered from the swaying caboose, both hands up. In that second, without thinking, I leapt up into the air and flew toward Abhi, tackling her out of the roaring train's path.

Everything happened in slow motion. Abhi and I flew through the air on our sides like twin missiles. All the while a shocked Abhi looked at me with her terrified gray eyes, and I looked back, strong and steady, as we flew together.

"Leave that poor girl alone, Delacruz!" Coach Ostraticki bellowed.

The crowd, who'd until that moment been hypnotized by dunking Coach Ostraticki, spun around at once to the horror of the train barreling straight for them.

They parted like the Red Sea, the train cutting a straight line for the dunking booth. Coach Ostraticki's eyes widened. Franticly, he blew his whistle, waving his hands for Blythe to stop.

"I can't stop this crazy thing!" Blythe screamed, gripping the steering wheel, a rush of wind blowing her conductor hat off.

"AHHHHHH!" The train passengers screamed.

Thankfully, the train slowed a little when it sank into the swampy grass around the tank.

"HOLD ON!" Blythe yelled.

With a loud crash, the lawn mower plowed into the dunking booth, knocking a wide-eyed Coach Ostraticki off his dunking bench! *Ku-splash!* Waves of water shot out of the dunking booth tank. The water in the tank had absorbed the bulk of the impact.

After all these years, it took a runaway train to finally dunk Coach Ostraticki. He pressed his face against what was left the clear plastic tank, looking at the mayhem, eyes bulging. Bubbles escaped his yelling mouth as he saw a crack grow in the tank. Panicked, he swam to the top. *C-RRR-ACK! SNAP!* The rest of the tank water broke through, rushing and spilling over the train and its stunned passengers. Coach Ostraticki looked like a river rafter as he passed over Blythe and the passengers, his whistle blowing a sad, wet sound.

The smell of chlorine wafted through the air as the train motor steamed and hissed.

In all the commotion, none of us had noticed poor Mrs. Darling swirling around in the panicked, crowd. Actually, you couldn't see Mrs. Darling—just her shoes poking out from beneath the cascarone tower, somehow still balancing the delicate eggs.

Mrs. Darling's tower teetered.

"I've got it . . . I've got it," she sang from behind an endless stack of eggs.

Mrs. Darling's tower tottered.

No idea what was in front of her, Mrs. Darling kept walking ahead. She had become a Jenga-game-gone-wrong and rocked forward and back. "I've . . . got . . ." Mrs. Darling's voice was still loud, but it began to quiver. Her sandals took a big step backward. Somehow she slipped on a large piece of plastic that had broken off the dunk tank. Her feet began surfing across the muddy mess—fast, but the rest of Mrs. Darling and the stacks of cascarones didn't.

"OH, MYYYY!" Mrs. Darling bellowed as her feet finally stopped sliding and shot up in the air. Her pink sandals flew off, and the stacks of cascarones catapulted from her hands high above the muddy field. In the air, the eggs began crashing into one another with such great force that their thin shells shattered and their confetti burst free. The shocked crowd looked up to see thousands of crushed cascarones flying through the air, like a confetti cannon had gone off at a Spurs basketball game.

"Ooh!" Helpless, the soaked passengers threw their hands up to block the shower of out-of-control cascarones that were tumbling and crashing over them.

Bits of confetti and eggshells floated down like colorful snow, mixing with the dunk-tank water, coating the passengers with bits of brightly colored paper and eggshell, making them look as if they were covered in pixilated tattoos.

Lying on the ground, even Abhi and I got covered with confetti.

What happened next was unbelievable.

From the back of the train, a confetti-coated El Pollo Loco jumped to his feet, spit a stream of water from his mouth like a fountain, and shouted, "Again! Let's go AGAIN! That was the best ride ever!"

CHAPTER 29

PAY ATTENTION TO WHAT'S IN FRONT OF YOU

I stood and reached out my hand to a dazed Abhi, lying on the field. She gripped mine tightly as I pulled her up.

"Are you okay, Abhi?" I steadied her with my hand on her shoulder.

"I think so." She brushed grass and confetti off her shirt and arms. "Thank you, Zack."

I stood with Abhi and watched a speckled and soaked Coach Ostraticki help Mrs. Darling up, while Nurse Patty made sure no one was hurt.

"What happened?" Abhi touched a small cut on her cheek.

"The train lost control and was about to run you over." I looked right in her eyes this time, as Cliché had said. Paying attention to what's in front of me was easy because Abhi's eyes kept me there. "I had to push you out of the way."

"I see." Abhi paused, rubbing her arm.

We stared at the debris all over the field. People climbed off the train, soaked and coated, but okay.

"I'm sorry I knocked you down, though." I gulped. "I didn't know what else to do."

I wasn't sure what to say next.

Blythe and her dad walked by.

We turned and watched Mr. Balboa side-hug his shivering daughter. Blythe bent down and picked up some of the shreds of her cardigan, coated with mud and confetti. "I need a new sweater." She bawled on her Dad's shoulder.

"Anything you want, baby." Mr. Balboa held on tight. "I'm just so glad everyone's all right."

I rocked back and forth, heal to toe. "I've also been meaning to thank you, Abhi, for saving me from being trampled to death on cinnamon roll day. You're a real shero."

Abhi beamed—and *beamed* wasn't just another word to use instead of *smiled*. She actually beamed, like the sun. "Well, we're even now, aren't we?"

"Sure." I shrugged my right shoulder. And the way she looked back at me, I think she thought I was beaming too. And it was this great moment: I didn't hear or see anything else around us. I was just there. Abhi and I.

Which is why it was even more shocking when Dilum suddenly shoved between us. "Why you little . . ."

"Stop it!" Abhi interrupted. "This boy was just trying to get me out of the way of the train, so I wouldn't get flattened."

Dilum eyed me for a few seconds. Then he nodded and stuck out his hand.

We shook. He gripped way too hard and pulled me close. With his other hand he poked two fingers at his eyes, reminding me he'd be watching.

I nodded that I understood.

Dilum walked off, yelling to one of his friends, "Hey, wait up!"

"I'm sorry." Abhi said. "Dilum is a very protective big brother."

"I understand." I said.

"You do?" Abhi looked at me.

"No, not really." I shrugged. "I don't have any brothers or sisters."

"Brothers can be such a pain." Abhi smiled. "But it would be lonely without any."

I nodded and took a deep breath. "But I'm the one who isn't done saying, 'I'm sorry.'"

Abhi tilted her head. "You already did."

"But I didn't say I was sorry about the whole dodgeball thing. I never meant to hurt you then either." My voice got louder and faster. "I never even tried to hit you."

She nodded.

"I'm not that good of shot." I touched my chest. "Ask anybody."

"It's true." El Pollo Loco ran past us, aggressively pointing his thumbs at the ground. "He's the worst."

"Hey," I snapped at José, "can you give us a minute?"

"Chill out, Captain Underpants," José said, moon-walking off. "I'll catch you on the flipside."

Abhi pulled her hair behind her ears. Even the confetti looked good on her.

"It was a total accident." I ran my hand over my head. "I was trying to miss you on purpose but not look like I was throwing the game. But I'm so bad at dodgeball that I can't even miss right. I felt so bad that I knocked you flat on your first day. But every time I tried to talk to you, everything would get all messed up. I'm so sorry I didn't say I was sorry."

"I guess I accept your apology then for not apologizing." Abhi nodded, giggling. "And I also forgive you for being a terrible shot."

But I wasn't done yet.

"And I'm sorry for being such a goofball in the cafeteria with my pants and saying so much stupid stuff. I just wanted to get to know you, that's all." Once I started, I couldn't stop apologizing.

Abhi smiled. "It's okay. Some of my best friends are goofballs."

All I had had to do was be honest. It felt good. It was like everything was okay and we could just talk. Except for one thing: I didn't know what else to say after I apologized. I hadn't thought that through. My mind started to spin like a hamster on a wheel. But then I stopped it. I took a breath. I remembered: pay attention to what's in front of you.

I looked right at Abhi, searching through my brain to find something to say, but my search engine came back: "no results found."

She waited for me to talk. What was I supposed to say? I had never gotten that far. I'd waited so long to finally talk to Abhi that once I had the chance, I didn't know what else to say.

Abhi broke the silence. "I thought you hated me because I was different."

"No." My jaw dropped. "I don't hate you. Not at all."

We stood in the silence of our misunderstandings. Then I said something really lame. "I think people from Minnesota are fine."

Abhi cracked a smile.

#HumorSaves.

"That's good to know." Abhi swallowed a laugh.

She looked back at me—right in my eyes. "I think you saved my life."

I smiled.

Then, Abhi walked up to me and gave me a hug.

After a few seconds, El Pollo Loco tapped on my shoulder, interrupting my hug with Abhi. "May I cut in?"

"Huh?"

"It's okay." Abhi said, turning. "He's my friend too." She patted José's shoulder.

José quickly touched his head on Abhi's shoulder. "Awww, thanks!" Then he ran off.

I squinted. "We're friends?"

"Of course we are, Zack. Besides, I'm new here and I could obviously use more friends." She motioned her head at El Pollo Loco, who was now running around the field like the crazy chicken he would always be.

"Bwalk, Bwalk!" He squawked. "I am El Pollo Loco, the official mascot of the Fall Fiesta-val. *BW—AAAALK!"*

"Unauthorized mascot, I might add." Mr. Akins used his bullhorn again.

Things were getting back to normal.

Marquis ran up, a rubber chicken still in his hand. "Zack, are you okay?"

"Yes, *we* are." I answered, smiling. "Marquis, this is my friend, Abhi." I motioned to Abhi.

"Nice to meet you, Marquis." Abhi reached out her hand.

"Same here," Marquis shook her hand and looked back and forth at Abhi and me, trying to figure out what had happened while he was gone.

"Marquis is my best friend." I patted his shoulder.

"Well, any friend of Zack's is a friend of mine," Abhi smiled. "After all, he saved my life."

"What?" Marquis asked.

"I'll tell you all about it on the way home."

"M'man Zack will always surprise you." Marquis flashed a grin.

"Marquis!" Cliché ran up between Marquis and Abhi. "I was so scared. Are you okay?"

"Yeah! I was looking for you too," Marquis said. "I'm glad you're okay. I was worried about you."

"You *were*?" Cliché clutched her chest, catching her breath. "That's the nicest thing I've heard all day."

A confetti-coated El Pollo Loco joined the group. "You did Champ the Choo-Choo proud today, Zack." El Pollo Loco slapped me on the back, leaving a wet confetti print.

"Thanks, José," I said, attempting to brush myself off.

"You may call me El," José held up a finger. "All my friends do."

"El," I said.

Abhi snorted, which caused us all to crack up.

"Ahhhhh!" Janie suddenly appeared, her hands pressed together in a triangle, observing, nodding. "It all happened just as I predicted." She bushed her hands together. "Madame Bustamante's work here is done." She held out her hands as if she had made it all happen. And as I thought about it, she had.

I stared at Janie in her fortune-telling getup for a few seconds. And then I did it. I told the truth. It had been right in front of me for a while now. "And here's my friend Janie." It confused Janie at first, but she recovered quickly and curtsied. Yes, curtsied. She was still Janie.

"Davy Crockett Middle School is one crazy place." Abhi nodded, looking around at everyone, coated and stumbling in the wet mess. "It wasn't like this in Minnesota."

"Welcome to my world." I motioned at the whole field, the whole big wonderful mess.

Abhi smiled.

Behind Marquis and Cliché, I spotted a cascarone on the ground. I don't know how, but in all the crashing and flooding and panicking, this one cascarone had survived—completely whole and undamaged.

If that wasn't luck, then I didn't know what was. And there it was—right in front of me. I walked over, leaned down, and gently scooped up the only surviving cascarone. I skulked up behind Marquis and Cliché, who were deep in conversation. I lifted the last cascarone above Marquis's head and brought it down, smashing it and rubbing the mess into my best friend's hair.

"Not my 'fro!" Marquis pulled back, pushing me away with his hands, but the deed was done.

'It looks good on you." Cliché smiled, turning her head. "Very festive. And it was free!" Cliché high-fived me. "I think there will be enough cascarone bits everywhere for us to remember this day for a long time to come."

The day I finally got to know Abhi, I thought. We were even friends. She'd said so. I wanted to remember that for sure.

I have to admit I did smash the first egg, but it was Janie who first picked up a handful of the wet confetti mess and flung it into the middle of our group.

Then, of course, José—or El—swiped up a handful of muddy cascarone bits off the ground and heaved it at me. And suddenly we hurled cascarone chum like we were in a food fight in a movie. Laughing, throwing, and accidentally bringing in new victims and throwers, the cascarone fight spread like chicken pox.

"*Studens*, please cease and desist with the all cascarone-related nonsense. *SQUEEEEAL*." Mr. Akins blasted on his bullhorn.

"What about *other* kinds of nonsense?" the cascarone-coated El questioned.

Mr. Akins's sighed into the bullhorn, which screeched so loud he dropped it on the wet grass.

"Mic drop!" El yelled.

We laughed. Because we knew the nonsense would never really stop. Not today. Not tomorrow. Not ever.

Not at Davy Crockett Middle School, home of the Fighting Alamos, where the school mascot was a building. Not with Madame Bustamante and El Pollo Loco and Cliché and Marquis and me.

And now Abhi.

Things will always be happening. Some may seem like good luck and others like bad luck. But it really isn't about all that. It's about what you do with what's in front of you. That's what makes life happen. And everything may not turn out exactly the way we want, but it can still be good.

Like today.

And that's enough.

As long as I'm paying attention to what's in front of me, I'll be ready for whatever crazy thing comes next.

IN GRATITUDE

One thing Zack discovers in *Just My Luck* is that there is so much wonderful stuff going on in the world all the time, and it's right in front of him, if he'll only get out of his worrying mind. Writing Zack's stories takes me out of my worrying mind and gives me hope. If I make a child laugh, I feel important and I stop worrying, if only for a moment. I have to thank my readers, young and old. It's been fun sharing Zack's stories with you and hearing your own. Kudos to the librarians, administrators, teachers, and booksellers, who work tirelessly to get books like the Zack Delacruz series in the hands of those who need it most. You make this work so worthwhile.

Thanks to all of you who share your lives, on a daily basis, and take me out of my worrying mind and into the beautiful world: Lisa, Gino, Sam, Wiley, Monica, Heather, Edie, Ricky, Brandy, and of course, always my first editor and best friend, Terry. Always.

I am grateful to the children's book writing community. Your kindness and grace have meant the world to me. I hope to keep connecting, sharing, and presenting with you for years to come. Thank you for inviting me in. I need you.

None of this is possible without the keen insight of my editor, Brett Duquette. He's a cheerleader and smarty-pants extraordinaire. Andrea Miller your art is only surpassed by your kindness and class. Thanks to my agent Roseanne Wells, who is a great reader of early drafts. I am so lucky to get to work with the Sterling Publishing family. It doesn't even feel like work (most of the time). Lauren, Sari, Theresa, Hanna, Chris, Scott, Irene, and Trudi, where would I be without your tireless support? Thank you.

And last, thank you for reading, readers. I'll see you again real soon, maybe in between the pages or in person. Either way, stay in touch!

—Jeff Anderson

ABOUT THE AUTHOR

JEFF ANDERSON is the author of *Zack Delacruz: Me and My Big Mouth*, *Mechanically Inclined*, *Everyday Editing*, *10 Things Every Writer Needs to Know*, and *Revision Decisions*. *Zack Delacruz: Just My Luck* is the wacky sequel to his debut middle grade novel. Jeff grew up in Austin, Texas, and learned to love writing by journaling and crafting stories to entertain his friends over the phone. A former elementary and middle school teacher, Jeff travels to schools across the country, working with teachers and students to discover joy and power in the writing process. Jeff lives with his partner, Terry, and their dogs, Carl and Paisley. Find out more about Jeff at writeguy.net or follow him on Twitter @writeguyjeff. Jeff lives in San Antonio, Texas.